THE ROSE BATH RIDDLE
THE COMPLETE CASES OF JIGGER
MASTERS, VOLUME 2

THE ROSE BATH RIDDLE

THE COMPLETE CASES OF JIGGER MASTERS, VOLUME 2

ANTHONY RUD

ILLUSTRATED BY
JOSEPH A. FARREN

COVER BY
C.C. BEALL

POPULAR PUBLICATIONS · 2022

TABLE OF CONTENTS

THE ROSE BATH RIDDLE

*It Was Murder in a Strange Form That
Eluded Even Jigger Masters, for This
Murder Was a Sinister Phantom That
Slipped Through Bolted Doors*

1

TWENTY GRAINS A SECOND

NO MORE THAN half of the sixty or seventy couples expected for some part of the long week-end, were gathered on the terraced lawn at Friday midnight. But faces were gay. Gowns were gracious and lovely. Men, some of whom had smiled little through nearly four years of nerve-rack and strain, were toasting anything or anyone in slender glasses of the French wine of Simon Corlaes.

As soon as the signal was given, they would be ready for anything, from love to leap frog. A hush of expectancy was descending. Stella Mallen, their hostess, and Simon Corlaes, her half-brother, had welcomed them as they arrived. Corlaes, in appearance a sort of rubbery, bunch-muscled satyr, was going to speak to them all for a moment. He had set up a tiny stage there among the yews. Soft floodlights played upon its bare boards.

"Quite like the old reprobate, to throw one last sneer, like an arrow into the air," drawled Lacey Glendon, a swarthy, lean man in his thirties.

"Probably has a dozen State troopers lurking in the cedars, though. A brave old boy, my esteemed uncle—when he is sure there's no danger threatening him!"

A blond, baby-faced girl at his side giggled audibly, then

Corlaes squealed and
Masters stopped abruptly

shot a glance at her mother, standing at Lacey Glendon's left.

The elder woman's lips tightened in disapproval.

"Are you sober tonight, Lacey?" she inquired with deceptive mildness. "Nerves all ragged? Temper short? Try a glass of that Château Yquem—"

"Not at all, Mrs. Gunter," laughed Glendon easily. "Neither drunk nor sober, neither happy nor sad. Just curious. Unk has some mysterious plan. I saw him with H_2O pottering around in the laboratory this afternoon. They—"

"H_2O?" echoed Eloise Gunter, the slender blonde. "That's water, isn't it?"

"Not in this case. Incomparable Henry Handley Oliver, I meant. He's a young man you must meet sometime, Eloise…"

*... A man in chauffeur's livery, and a man in
white flannels moving feebly on the concrete*

Lacey Glendon's velvety voice held a hint of sarcasm,
well veiled. "You may have seen him today—or at some
time earlier. He is Unk's chief laboratory assistant. They
say those krypton gas process patents ought to have been
taken out in his name. But of course that's old scandal.
Stout fella."

"You shouldn't talk that way about your Uncle Simon,"
reproved Mrs. Penrhyn Gunter, frowning slightly. "He is a
great man, and not to be judged by the same standards—"

"A rich man, Mrs. Gunter," amended Lacey, "and therefore not even to be arrested, let alone judged. But look,
there he comes, bouncing along like a monkey. Still in his
blue-devil suit."

Eloise Gunter's laugh was lost in the boisterous hilar-
ity of welcome to the host. Many of the guests assembled
hated or envied Simon Corlaes. A few were big enough to

despise him. Yet there was an undeniable fascination about the man. Physically ugly, a contortionist and an athlete despite his considerable paunch and his fifty-two years, he could have had their rapt attention just the same if he had been a penniless charlatan, instead of being one of the five richest men on Long Island.

His overwhelming chest laugh booming out above the excited clamor of his guests, the short-statured Simon Corlaes made his way rapidly toward the lighted stage. He nudged a woman or two on the way, earning frowns from their escorts—though not from the women.

The platform was raised three feet above the smooth terrace. A row of footlights, shielded from the eyes of the guests by a chromium reflector, added ten inches to this.

Simon Corlaes bounded up, touching nothing with his hands. Then he turned, grinning widely, and held up both blue arms for silence.

Even his finger-nails were dyed indigo. A blue skull-cap with short projecting horns, hid his sparse gray hair. A professional make-up artist had done his countenance, accomplishing Mephistophelian wonders with unpromising material. Satin tights and doublet revealed all of his muscled ugliness, as well as his paunch. Grotesquely he seemed to be a trifle hump-backed, though everyone knew this was not the case.

"Friends and enemies!" he boomed in salutation, as the tinkle and chatter subsided. "I am the blue devil of strict sobriety. I have ruled during the past years of business depression. Now those who know say positively that my reign is at an end!"

A clamorous cheer, punctuated by doubting cries, greeted this. His hands raised again.

"I am content!" he chortled. "I bid you farewell. My work is done!"

"I'll say it is!" gritted one pale-faced guest in the audience. But his comment was lost in what happened instantly.

There came a loud hiss of escaping gas or vapor. A white cloud of steamy fog swept up from the region of the speaker's ankles. It enveloped him completely for seconds… half a minute.

Then the hissing ceased. The mild summer breeze, mounting upward to the terrace from the moonlit waters of Long Island Sound, blew the vapor gently aside.

There, fully revealed to their startled gaze, was the same man—but now he was *bright scarlet from head to foot!*

"Shucks," said Lacey Glendon in an undertone, "I can do the same thing with litmus paper!"

Undoubtedly most of the guests realized that the seeming miracle was the merest child's play for a chemistry wizard like Simon Corlaes. Yet it was impressive.

"And now I am with you again!" he boomed, ending the sentence with a chuckle. "Your old Devil, the one you loved in days of prosperity! On with the dance! Let joy be unconfined!"

And with that he bowed, leapt down amid the storm of laughter, cheers and jeers, and ran for the wide veranda of Corlaes Manor.

THREE MINUTES LATER, perspiring, chuckling and a trifle out of breath, Simon Corlaes unlocked the door of his private apartment on the second floor of the southeast wing. He would have to get this stuff off his face and hands quickly, bathe, dress in white flannels and blue serge jacket, and get out among 'em again. Several mighty pretty girls present. New buds on the branch. Well, Simon was the man to appreciate their fragrance… ha!

On his way to the immense and luxurious private bath he suddenly stopped with one foot in air. Then he put it down slowly to the rug, and stared. Visibly he seemed to deflate, to lose all of his rotund jollity.

There before him, sprawled face downward on the rug, lay Edward Green, his personal valet!

With a sound oddly like the doubting whimper of a very small dog, Simon stepped forward and knelt. The valet's head looked strangely flattened in the back.

No blood showed, yet Simon put his hand there first.

"Oh, my God!" he exclaimed sharply, jerking away and glancing down at his scarlet fingers as if blood might have appeared against the redder hue of the chemical. The bones of the servant's skull had been crushed, over a surface as large as a man's hand!

"No doubt *he's* dead!" breathed Simon through chattering teeth. He leapt up like a monkey, and ran for the house phone on one of his tables.

"That you, Sorenson? Oh, Walker. Well, Walker, something's terrible here! Ed Green has been killed! I found him lying dead here in the living room of my suite. Yes, dead! Head all squashed. Ugh! Send Sorenson up to me. And you—you call the police department at Mineola. No, I don't think the State troopers. I don't know. Anyway, I've got to get this acid stuff off my skin. Green's dead—and *some*body killed him!"

Simon Corlaes was shaking. Death sickened him.

That horrible time he had found his own brother a suicide, it had taken Simon days to recover.

Now his skin was stinging, his eyes watering from the fumes of the chemicals. Half-blinded, he ran into the bathroom, stripping off his doublet, his skullcap, then his tights. Pouring a gill of ammonia into a basin of hot water, keeping his eyes tight shut, he swashed his wrists and face generously. Then he dried hastily with a towel, glimpsing his pudgy face, now mottled red and blue.

A smearing with cold cream came then. When Sorenson the butler appeared, with one of the maids following on tiptoe, Simon was stark naked, ruthlessly scrubbing the color from his hands onto a Turkish towel.

The maid got one horrified look, and fled screaming. To the end of her days she would have nightmares of that horribly mottled face, that bulgy naked man standing above the dead body of old Ed Green…

But Simon paid no attention, except to have the butler lock the door. Then came hasty dressing, with Sorenson of very little use.

A second and far graver shock was waiting Simon Corlaes, when he walked in front of the chiffonier in his bedroom, tying his white silk cravat. There on top of the chiffonier, was a typed note, propped up some way so he could not miss it when he came to dress. He stared at it.

It read tersely:

WHEN THE SAND GRAINS STOP RUNNING,
YOU WILL DIE!

He seized the single sheet, with trembling fingers. Then

his eyes dilated, and a soundless gasp burst from his lips. There on the chiffonier was an old-fashioned hour-glass, two-thirds of the sand grains already descended from the upper chamber to the lower.

"Twenty grains a second," flashed through Simon's frightened mind. He recalled with terrible clarity that other hour-glass, the one which had been on the desk in front of his dead brother, Alfred.

"But Alfred k-killed himself," stuttered Simon. "I won't do that!"

Up-ending the hour-glass, so the sands would have forty minutes to go in the opposite direction, Simon seized the glass and the typewritten note. He muttered something incoherent to Sorenson, who stared wonderingly, then dashed out of the suite, to the stairs, down—

And then he froze, gasping and crouching at the end of the stair balustrade. There in the hallway near the main entrance of the manor, stood two men. *The two men on earth he had most reason to fear.*

Young Marshall Corlaes was supposed to be Simon's own son. For months Marshall had not set foot inside the house, and old Simon had not as much as set eyes upon him. The last time had been a horror to Simon. Marshall Corlaes, infuriated beyond all reason, had struck him down; and might right then have killed him if Ed Green, the valet, had not interfered.

The other man was Stanley Kershaw. A strange, vindictive old fellow—with plenty reason to be vindictive. How did he get here? Who invited him? Was he the murderer of Ed Green?

The pair of Simon's enemies pretended to be unaware

of his presence. He crouched lower, black eyes darting about in desperation. Every shred of his gayety and apelike animal spirits had vanished. He was a hunted man, frightened of his own precious skin. His knees began to quake beneath him.

Of a sudden he took a chance. He whirled about the newel post and darted to a rear door. There he gained the end of the veranda. Down the short flight of stairs. Out to the garage as fast as swift, silent steps would take him, glancing back over his shoulder in ever mounting apprehension...

In the long garage, shrinking away from the chauffeur who aroused from a doze to proffer his services, Simon Corlaes took a big convertible roadster. As the doors swung wide he stepped on the gas. The two-toned horn sounded a signal for the peglegged gatekeeper a quarter mile away.

Then, gaining Highway 25A, Simon turned sharply left and trod on the gas. He was bound for the village of Biskra Harbor. Bound for the home of a queer man. One Simon had deemed a fanatic or charlatan. One who ten months earlier had persisted to the point of annoyance in claiming that Alfred Corlaes never in the wide world had shot himself.

Perhaps that fool private detective really knew something, after all!

2

A JOB FOR JIGGER MASTERS

J.C.K. MASTERS ROUSED slowly and with some reluctance from sleep, at the gentle shaking of his shoulder by Mitsui, his Japanese servant.

Jigger Masters was a six-foot man clad only in the lower half of a pair of white cotton pyjamas. He was a lean man, with tousled black hair worn long. Coarse hair, gleaming with vitality, and as hard to comb as so much waved fine wire.

Jaw both long and large, nose flaring at the nostrils, wide mouth full of strong teeth set unevenly in the lower jaw, and ears which no stretch of the imagination could call modest and retiring, made him frankly homely of countenance. Small grin wrinkles at the eye corners, and the hazel eyes themselves, holding small flecks of gold in the irises, redeemed the face, however. No men at all and few women remembered that they thought him ugly, ten minutes after meeting him.

"Oh-h—you, Mitsui. What's up?"

Masters sat up, swinging his long legs to the rug. He rubbed his eyes, then reached to a bed table for a paper packet of cigarettes. He scratched a match, and puffed.

"Crazy man downstaih. Come-see you," reported Mitsui,

unemotionally. "Ring bell. Toot ho'n. Jump up-an'-down allasame monkey. Give me ten dollah. Crazy."

Masters grinned and got to his feet, donning slippers and the upper half of his pyjamas.

"All right. If he's a client I'll be glad to see him, even in the middle of the night. Tell him—did he give a name, Mitsui?" Masters reached for a blue lounging robe.

"Oh-ya. I fo'get. Name is Simon Corlaes."

"Simon—hm!" The smile faded, and Masters straightened. "Well, well, then I was right!" he commented.

He had come to believe the Corlaes family a queer one—and one in which crime was as certain to appear sometime, as dandelions in a newly seeded lawn.

They had not accepted his suggestion in respect to the death of Alfred, though. He had followed the ruthless career of the two Corlaes brothers, and knew that cowardice and cruelty were strongly blended in both. Such men inevitably make enemies. Alfred Corlaes had never committed suicide.

Masters entered the library where his visitor was pacing the floor. All of the lights were ablaze; Simon Corlaes had pulled down the opaque window shades as well as the lighter ones, and snapped on the wall fixtures in addition to the ceiling lamps. He still held the hour-glass clutched in his left hand, as though it were his only hold on precious life. He was jumpy, palpably trembling, and his face had the gray-green pallor of seasickness.

"Ah, Mr. Masters! I'm glad you are here! They're after me!" he exclaimed. "Here, read that!" He thrust forward a rumpled sheet of paper, on which was the typed message he had found propped against the hourglass.

"No one can bother you here," assured Masters, after a look at the paper, and the glint of a grim smile at the childish manner this rich man held on to the hour-glass. "Have a chair. Oh, yes, that's the hour-glass. Sands still running, I see."

"I—I have turned it," admitted Simon, without the faintest hint of shame. "There are radio torpedoes, you know. All sorts of ways of employing vibration, or the cessation of vibration—"

"To be sure," nodded Masters casually. "Let me see the fiendish thing." He took it and studied it, amused contempt in the hazel eyes at sight of a multitude of sweaty finger-prints and thumbprints clouding the glass. No use dusting it for a sign of an intending murderer; Simon Corlaes had ruined that slight chance.

The typed letter, though, might not be as bad. Masters laid it aside for future consideration. He touched a hidden button. When Mitsui appeared, silent and impassive, Masters mentioned Scotch and Vichy—the Scotch for his new client. A moment later the drinks were poured, and Simon took his neat, and without appearing to notice he had been given half a highball glass. It soon had a calming effect, though.

"Well, even if you forgot to turn it, the sands would keep going for some time," said Masters. "I think we can put it aside, while you tell me all you know about this business from the beginning."

He reached over with apparent carelessness to the table, and set down the hour-glass. What Simon Corlaes was unable to see from where he sat, was that Masters, in putting down the ominous hour-glass, set it on its side. The grains of sand ceased to flow!

With four ounces of Sandy MacDonald whisky under his belt, the millionaire was able to remain seated now. He still fidgeted, and his hands moved restlessly, though.

Simon was in no shape for a coherent recital. It was not until Masters began questioning him rather impatiently that the truly serious happening of the evening came to light.

A choked expletive came from the detective then.

"You mean to sit there and tell me—just as an unimportant aside, Corlaes—that while you have been shivering and shuddering over the fright you've had, a man actually lies dead, *murdered,* in your home? And that the police are probably now in charge, with you a fugitive somewhere unknown?"

"I suppose I was in a panic," the millionaire muttered. "I remembered that you said Alfred was not at all the sort to kill himself; that he must have been murdered. I—lost my head, I guess."

"Well, find it quickly now! Look here!" Masters gestured him to the table. "While we have been talking, the hour-glass you brought has been lying there—on its side. The sands have stopped long ago. Do you suppose that you can buck up, and realize that there is no bomb waiting to explode when those sands stop?"

Simon wiped the cold perspiration from his forehead. "Yes, I can—now. I want you to take charge of my end, and find out who sent me this threat. The death of Ed Green is just an ordinary thing. The police can take care of that."

"No murder is an ordinary thing," Masters responded,

and excused himself to go and dress. He reflected that the whole situation bore the earmarks of a thorough mess. A servant killed, the master threatened, and at the time of the happening some fifty or sixty guests on the estate, twelve or fifteen servants up and around, a forty-piece orchestra playing, and some professional entertainers with rooms in the manor house. How could the police or any number of detectives sort out such an angle?

He dressed, instructing Mitsui to notify Barnes and Gildersleeve, his assistants, and departed.

WHEN MASTERS AND Simon Corlaes drove into the estate grounds and into the garage, no chauffeur was in evidence. Masters supposed the man was out with one of the machines which was missing from the ten-car line-up.

"Have you only the one chauffeur?" he asked sharply.

"Yes, only one—now," responded the millionaire, his nervousness vastly increased by returning to the estate. "The depression, you know. Wouldn't look well to have more."

"Well, then, take this," said Masters, repressing his contempt. He handed to Corlaes his .32-20 revolver. "Don't get scared and shoot without cause, but defend yourself if it looks necessary. I won't be long."

"Are you going to l-leave me?" stammered Corlaes.

"Only till I see the decks cleared inside. Then I'll get you up to your rooms, and make a regular fort out of them. Just sit still here for perhaps ten minutes. You'll be safe. That's why I drove right into the garage."

Masters walked swiftly back to the house and went in. He found that much of the ground-clearing necessary before a police inquiry could really get under way, had been done. Lieutenant Selwyn Connor, of the Mineola police, was in charge, and he was an exceedingly serious man. This kind of a society mob was more dangerous than sweated dynamite to handle.

Few if any of the guests had dreamt of going home from the party before dawn, at the earliest. A dozen people, indeed, were house guests. Yet within five minutes of being herded in from the terraced lawns by blue-coated police-men, chased off the dance floor, and routed out of the wooded nooks where the flirtatious had been watching moonlight on the Sound, every single one was clamoring to go home.

What did it matter to any of them that a valet, whom few of those assembled even had seen, had died mysteri-ously? These were people of importance. Or, if they were not really important, they wished to seem so.

As far as his abilities extended, the excellent police lieu-tenant had exhibited swift competence. Photographing of the corpse and the living room of the suite occupied by Simon Corlaes, the work of the fingerprint men, and many routine details had been completed upstairs. Lieu-tenant Connor, wondering grimly to himself if the eccen-tric owner of this place simply had not run amok, smashing down his valet for some real or fancied fault, shrank from the ordeal of interviewing the guests.

Still, it had to be done, or he would get cynical censure in the press. Setting his wide, competent jaw, Connor, in company of the County Medical Examiner, was actually descending the stairs, when Jigger Masters walked in—alone.

"Nasty job, Cortelyou," Connor was saying from

between taut lips. "Probably will mean *my* job, no matter how well or how badly I handle it. Well, we die but once. Hello—is that Masters? Lord, I wish—"

The detective nodded briefly.

"I have news for you, Connor," he said quietly. "Simon Corlaes came for me. I left him outside, but I'll bring him in as soon as possible. There's more to this than just the murder of Edward Green, though that's bad enough."

"More?" said the lieutenant slowly. "Just what do you mean by that? Dr. Cortelyou says the killing is probably the work of a maniac. Has Simon Corlaes gone mad?"

"Not that way, at any rate, I feel sure."

"Sane enough to come back, anyhow," put in the medical examiner dryly. "We thought he might have skipped."

Masters, with due deference to the law, asked a few brief questions concerning these people, some of whom were raising their voices in angry, rhetorical protest.

"Heavens, I suppose it means question every one," said Connor resignedly.

"If you'll allow a suggestion," interposed Masters quietly, "I think I can be of help."

"Oh, anything. What is it? You know how glad I am you're here." There was no doubt of the lieutenant's sincerity. His abilities, considerable as they were, did not lie in the field of crime analysis.

"Right," nodded Masters. "Then, take my word that this affair goes much deeper than a mere crime passionnel among servants. Simon Corlaes has received a letter threatening his life. I would do just this as a start. Make a list of all the guests here now, with their addresses. Warn each to hold himself in readiness to be called for questioning later.

Then let them go home. There are ten or twelve, I believe, who were to have stayed here over the week-end. Keep them here. Question every one of these, the host and host-ess, the orchestra, entertainers and all the servants right away concerning the list you make. Doubtless you will find that some names of visitors or others will come up, men or women who were here during the evening, and who left, for one reason or another. It will be simple routine for one of your men, but be sure to get that list absolutely *complete!*"

The lieutenant brightened. Advice of this kind from such a source was easy to take. He even improved a good bit upon the detective's hasty outline, dividing the work of recording guests and others among eight of his men. Thus it moved forward expeditiously; and much of the carping criticism from guests who felt themselves outraged, was avoided. Little by little the crowd thinned.

THE ORCHESTRA LEFT as a unit. Barring a few momen-tary absences for refreshments, it had been lacking none of its regular members at any time since taking its place out near the dance floor. But far more important was the fact that it had been a last-minute choice on the part of the hostess, Mrs. Stella Mallen. The players had not known they were coming out on Long Island until the very day of the engagement. There was almost no conceivable connec-tion between these musicians and an obscure member of the manor house staff of servants.

There was one entertainer, a youthful, lovely girl who had done a suite of Mexican dances in between the tangos of the guests. She called herself Alicante—Mexican Span-ish for "The Serpent"—and the complicated writhings of her dances, in which she interpreted Aztec festivals and human sacrifice, had made plain enough how she had won that name.

The dancer had never set foot before on Long Island. She did not know a soul at the gathering, except her own maid who had accompanied her. The latter was a middle-aged, kindly-faced woman, still handsome in a faded fashion.

One person at Corlaes Manor, though, had known Alicante—at least, had known her real name to be Dorothy Graham. By sheer chance, Marshall Corlaes had seen her in a previous appearance in Westchester. With a diffidence strange in that forthright young man, he had not pressed for an acquaintance, but had come as a guest to the party at which she appeared each time since.

Now when news of the murder stopped the orchestra and the dancer, Marshall Corlaes was at Alicante's side almost as soon as her maid. The latter helped with a negli-gee. Marshall looked hungrily into the dark brown eyes of the girl, who returned his almost articulate gaze with wonder. But then he turned away and was lost in the mill-ing crowd.

The dancer felt a strong impression that she had seen him somewhere before. And in that group of strangers, most of them angry or disgruntled now, she was glad of the warm feeling of safety the youth's gray-blue eyes had somehow brought to her.

The girl and her maid were told then that since they had planned to stay the night at Corlaes Manor, they must now retire to the room assigned to them. Questioning would come later.

Marshall Corlaes also was told to remain, though he had

no desire to so do. He protested to Lieutenant Connor, but the latter sternly commanded him to ask for a room. As a member of the family, it certainly was necessary for him to stay.

The youth's mouth straightened to a harsh line at that. He looked about for Simon Corlaes, but did not see him. Then he walked slowly to the house, and sought the hostess. Stella Mallen assigned him his old room, the one he had not occupied since the break with Simon Corlaes, months before. With a frowning shrug of acceptance he went to it, and shortly after that retired. When they wanted to ask fool questions, they would know where to find him.

THE TEN MINUTES mentioned by Masters dragged slowly by for Simon Corlaes. From the house could be heard a faint murmur of voices, probably the servants talking in the rear. Simon's senses, sharpened by his tenseness, became conscious of a drip-drip-dripping sound from over at the other side of the wide garage.

Was it blood?

He squeezed so hard on the butt of the little revolver that he almost fired it. The impulse was to reach forward to the dash of his car, and turn on the headlights again. But he feared to do that. Here in the darkness a murderer might suspect his presence, might even have seen him ride in; yet his exact spot on the seat of the car would be difficult to determine.

He tried to tell himself that the dripping sound was nothing but a radiator leak. And, ironically, that was the exact truth, though he never learned it.

From the pitch dark, probably at the side where Louis the chauffeur was wont to doze in a chair when waiting evening duty, came a rubbing sound—quite as though someone was crawling on all fours along the concrete.

A murderer, coming for him!

For a long moment Simon sat immobile, petrified with a terror which ran like the burning chill of some of his own liquefied gases through his arteries. Then from his throat came gibbering shriek upon shriek of disorganized, unreasoning fear.

From down there somewhere on the concrete floor had risen a ghastly, sobbing groan of a man in mortal pain!

Emerging to the rear veranda, Masters heard the voiced terror. He had borrowed a Colt automatic from Connor, and now, yanking this from his armpit sling, he dashed through the screen door, down the short flight of steps, and directly for the door of the dark garage.

Simon managed then to turn on the headlamps of his roadster. Flinging himself out of the machine, he cowered against the wall, revolver in his shaking hand.

Masters saw him, realized that this was only fright, so reached for the light switch. This turned on ten big ceiling lamps, hanging from cords in position so that they were above the hoods of those automobiles actually in the places assigned to them.

"What's wrong?" he cried sharply.

But Corlaes could not speak. He just managed to shake his head, so the pendent jowls wagged from side to side, and gesture down at the floor at some distance from him.

Then Masters himself heard it. From beyond the car which stood directly in front of him, came a dry, gasping sound as if someone labored for air!

Corlaes squealed; and the detective went with swift

caution around the fenders and front bumper. There he stopped abruptly. Slumped sidewise, so his head and right arm dragged over one arm of the steamer deck chair in which he dozed while waiting for a call to duty, was a man in chauffeur's livery. This was Louis Haines, and he was stone dead.

And beyond him on the greasy concrete, moving feebly, lay a hatless man in white flannels and blue jacket, a man whose cheek was red with his own blood and who most evidently was struggling now for a shred of consciousness!

3

THE GRAY SOCK CLUE

JIGGER MASTERS MADE a swift examination of the wounded man, who seemed to be suffering from a cut and contusion over his right eyebrow. He seemed dazed, weak, but not in serious danger.

The chauffeur was dead. The top of his skull was pulpy, the bone apparently smashed to small bits. But the skin was unbroken, not even a spot of blood appearing on his sandy hair.

Then Masters strode to the door.

"Don't let this alarm you further," he said cuttingly, to the millionaire, who still huddled fearfully against the wall. "I'm just summoning help."

With that he aimed the Colt pistol into the sod near his feet, and fired three shots.

A clamor of alarmed cries arose from the parking space around at the east side of the house. Here some of the guests, receiving speedy dismissal from Connor's men, had been about to drive away to their homes.

These guests came part way to the garage. Then discretion overcame their valor, and they hurried back. The sounds of their cars rapidly receding came to the detective's ears. If this were another mix-up, they preferred to get out of it and stay out of it, he supposed.

Two uniformed men arrived. These Masters told briefly of what he had found, asking one of them to fetch the lieutenant and Dr. Cortelyou.

The other policeman he asked to stay beside Corlaes, who had ventured forth far enough so he glimpsed the dead man and the fellow who groaned.

Masters got out of him the information that this was the chauffeur, Louis Haines, in the deck chair, and the other man was a nephew of Simon Corlaes, Lacey Glendon by name. Then Masters left his chicken-livered employer to the rather contemptuous attentions of the policeman, who sat him down on the running board of a car.

Over the hair and clothes of the lean, swarthy man whom Corlaes had named Lacey Glendon was sprinkled wet sand. Some of this was caught in the edges of the bruise on his forehead.

Casting about carefully, after placing a car cushion under the man's head, Masters came upon an explanation of the sand. Lying against the front wheel of a Packard coupé was a gray woollen sock, obviously of the sort worn for golf. It was small in size, short in length, and had a queer appearance of distortion.

It had been darned with gray wool in several places. Now the toe was broken out at the end. Wet sand adhered to the inside of the sock foot, and evidently had spilled out of the aperture at the toe when Glendon was struck.

"An ugly weapon, if the whole foot was filled with sand," said Masters to the policeman with Corlaes. "Must have weighed five or six pounds. An impromptu blackjack."

Lieutenant Connor, the medical examiner, and two other officers appeared abruptly then. With only a curious glance at Simon Corlaes, sitting huddled on the car running board, Dr. Cortelyou went at once to the body of the chauffeur.

Then, shrugging, but still wordless, he knelt and examined Lacey Glendon. He took the pulse twice, frowning, ran practiced fingers over the man's skull, and then stood up.

"Badly jarred. No fracture that I can find," he said. "Want to take him to the hospital, or put him to bed here? Dragging pulse—odd… He wasn't a dope user, was he?"

"Lacey?" asked old Simon vaguely. "I don't know. Probably he was… is… oh, I suppose we can find a place for him if he's not going to die. I don't like death."

"Few do," said the doctor dryly.

Under Masters' tactful direction, police escorted Simon Corlaes, and carried the limp and half-conscious Glendon into the house. Mounting the stairs in the rear, and thus avoiding guests, though not the staring, frightened servants, both men were taken upstairs to chambers.

Glendon was put to bed in the first chamber the police found unlocked, a small room normally part of a guest suite, but which could be bolted off to make a unit with its bath. A policeman was detailed to stay right in the room; and a physician was summoned from Biskra Harbor.

"IF HE REGAINS the ability to talk," said Masters to the officer, "I want to question him briefly at once. Tell the doctor that when he comes."

Before leaving the room he himself felt the wounded man's pulse, finding it slow.

"Fifty-one to the minute. For his height about seventy would be normal, wouldn't it, Dr. Cortelyou?"

The examiner sniffed. "That's an old man of thirty-five you have there," he said. "Eighty, with some flutter, would be more what you'd expect. He has the flutter," he concluded rather grimly.

Masters spent a long time bending over the forehead contusion and cut. The bleeding had stopped; and Cortelyou had not thought the cut itself merited stitches, being less than one inch long. During this examination the patient moved restlessly, and groaned. Though his eyes came open, their dull, vacant stare precluded any idea of questioning at the moment.

Searching the back and crown of the man's skull for a possible second bruise, the detective found nothing. He scowled as he turned away, motioning to the others to follow.

They went to the apartment of Simon, where one man was on guard in the locked room over the corpse of Edward Green, which lay now covered with a sheet.

The bedroom and magnificent bath lay beyond. They could be locked from the outside and bolted from the inside.

"You are going to be a virtual prisoner here for a time, Mr. Corlaes," said Masters, nodding for the trembling man to enter his own chamber.

"You don't mean—arrest?" stammered Corlaes, blinking. Evidently the thought had come to him in due time, that he himself might be suspected of this violence. He had been alone with Edward Green, and had given the alarm.

He had been out there in the garage, where another corpse and a wounded man had come to light…

Masters eyed him steadily. From the palpably overwrought condition of the millionaire it was difficult to suspect him. He had had opportunity, but scarcely the nerve or ability.

"Look here, Mr. Corlaes," he said. "It seems to me that you are forgetting my place in this matter. You called me to discover who it was sent you that hour-glass threat, and to protect you. I am going to try to see to it that no one menaces you in any way, until the police have done their work and caught the murderer of your servants. He may very well be the man you yourself have cause to fear—or the woman."

Simon paced up and down with long, springy steps, but looking more like an aged hunchback than ever, while Masters himself inspected every possible hiding place, and all the cupboards and clothespresses. The toothpaste, shaving brush, toothbrush, mouth lotions, and all the simple medicines in the bath cabinet he dumped into a wastebasket and handed to a policeman.

"Dump these out. Mr. Corlaes will get supplies of this sort, as well as all food and drink, and smokes, from Gildersleeve, one of my men."

At that moment Dr. Cortelyou, who had remained outside, came to the door to report that Barnes and Gildersleeve had phoned to say they would be around shortly. The medico also was anxious to take his own departure. Stretcher men were ready to take the bodies away, as soon as Masters declared himself satisfied. The inquest would be held the following day, at two o'clock in the afternoon.

Going out into the living room of the suite, listening until he heard the door of Corlaes' bedroom bolted behind him, Masters nodded to Cortelyou and approached the stiffened corpse of Edward Green.

"I want to make a cursory examination, Doctor," he said. "But of course I am depending upon your report. This was the cause of death?" He indicated the bashed-in skull. A few fragments of splintered bone had pushed through the scalp.

"As far as I can tell now, yes," said the examiner. "It looks to be plenty," he added dryly.

"In your opinion, could this be done with a sock full of wet sand?"

The medico frowned. "Not unless the old fellow was held down and literally pounded time and again!" he said. "One smash would never do it. That's why I hinted at insanity. At that time I thought—" He glanced toward the locked door of the bedroom.

"And the fracture sustained by that chauffeur Haines, seemed of the same nature?"

"Ye-es. Not so thorough a job, though. Haines probably lived a few minutes."

"And then the last one—that chap, Lacey Glendon," said Masters. He had finished with Edward Green, and drew the sheet again over the head. "Did that strike you as being the same sort of wound?"

The doctor scratched his chin, on which gray-brown bristles were beginning to call for a pre-breakfast shave.

"If it hadn't been for the sand, and the sock—" he began slowly.

"Exactly," snapped Masters, hazel eyes glinting. "What then?"

"Well," the doctor hesitated, "I might have thought it the result of a good stiff punch with a fist. If there had been a ring with some sort of a sharp setting, to make that scratch. It really wasn't much of a cut, and would scarcely have bled except it happened to slice through a network of capillaries."

"Good enough," nodded Masters. "I suppose, though, if the killer gathered up that wet sand on the beach, there might have been a nail or bit of glass in it."

"Yes, I hadn't thought of that."

Masters did not see any reason to tell him that a careful examination of the gray sock, and also the floor and the clothes of Lacey Glendon had failed to disclose any nail or the minutest particle of sharp material capable of making that scratch.

But Simon Corlaes, as Masters had noticed, wore a lodge signet ring on the little finger of his right hand!

4

TANGLED TRAILS

BY SIX O'CLOCK, when the servants produced a breakfast of sorts, Lieutenant Connor had augmented his force of men a second time, and had taken unofficial action in respect to Jigger Masters.

"You're in this anyhow," the police officer said. "You can protect Simon Corlaes better with the aid of my men than you can alone, however. And so, if you're willing, I want you to jump right in and take authority. Give me your orders, and I'll see they're carried out.

"You see, we haven't the facilities of a Metropolitan police force out here. Nassau County has excellent police in nearly every village; but as for detectives—"

Gravely enough, Masters agreed. It was his first job as a detective-executive; but from the first he had seen that—barring a simple and obvious explanation which might come to light in a few hours—a battery of investigators like so many hydraulic monitors wearing away stubborn cliffs containing small quantities of valuable ore, would be required.

"All right, Connor," he said. "I'm ready to start. I've got Gildersleeve taking care of old Simon. And, by the way, I'm going to let him rest till a little later. His wits are half-par-alyzed with fright."

"And Mr. Lacey Glendon doesn't seem to be able to understand, or to talk," frowned Connor. "One of the two of them surely ought to be able to put us on the right track."

"Is the list of guests complete? Did any get away before the alarm was spread?"

"Only one, as far as I have been able to make out," responded Connor, frowning slightly. "There was one man named Kershaw whom a good many people saw and recog-nized—he'd been associated with Alfred Corlaes, three or four years ago—who seems to have vanished. Just when, no one knows, though it must have been after that red-devil business.

Funniest part is that not even Oliver, the old man's assis-tant in the laboratory, knows where Kershaw came from. But doubtless Corlaes himself can tell us."

"Oliver is that red-haired man with glasses, they call H_2O, isn't he? Henry Handley Oliver?"

"Yes. As far as I can make out he's about halfway between the servants and the members of the family. Maybe he has some expectations under Simon's will. There's a thought for you, Jigger. Thanks, sezze"—and Connor grinned—"but I threw that in the wastebasket a week ago."

"Not at all," said Masters soberly. "But I'm here to make sure there's no need to look at Simon's will. There's trouble enough without that.

"Then, as soon as we eat, detail some of your men who can take preliminary statements to interviewing the servants. It would be a good groundwork if we had a signed timecard from each one, telling just where he or she was every minute from ten o'clock onward. This won't take the place of more serious questioning, but it will make any one that's inclined to hold back information, a little uneasy."

"I'll see to that, and question most of the men myself," promised Connor.

"Have you done anything about that gray sock?" asked the detective.

"Well, I still have it," the lieutenant responded. "It probably is the death weapon."

"Yes, probably the *death* weapon!" agreed Masters with peculiar, grim emphasis. "I could bear to know who owned the thing, though. Let's see it again."

When the broken-toed sock was brought, he held it up to the light, stretching the fabric and peering into it.

"Is it a boy's sock?" asked Connor. "If it belonged to our criminal, he couldn't be much over four feet high." He scratched the bristles on his chin vigorously.

"May I borrow it an hour or so? I want to have Barnes take it over to the laboratory for a few minutes."

"Why, of course. Only—I don't see—"

But Masters, summoning a quiet little man who looked like a failed stockbroker resigned to clipping hedges for a living, gave him a few low-voiced instructions. Placing the sock in the inside breast pocket of his neat jacket, Barnes hurried away.

BREAKFAST INTERVENED. MASTERS sat down to ripe grapefruit of the canned variety, excellent coffee, hot muffins, a pair of shad roe and crisped rashers of bacon. He granted Simon Corlaes a good cook, after that. Any staff of servants that could produce a meal fit to eat after such a disorganizing night, could have little guilt on its collective conscience.

After that, with blueprints of the manor house, he went up to the living room of Corlaes' suite, where Gildersleeve was seated, smoking a round-bowled, mahogany-colored meerschaum pipe.

"The patient is restin' easy," said the smoker, eyes twinkling as he looked up at his chief. "He chased me out, locked the door. I s'pose he went to sleep. I told him to holler when he wanted one of our special, wrapped-in-cellophane, hand-opened egg breakfasts. But he kinda gagged, an' said he'd never be hungry again. Just a little bit weak across the beltline for such a hellious old skirt-chaser, isn't he?"

Masters smiled, but did not reply directly.

"Leg it to Connor," he commanded. "I left a letter with him to be fingerprinted, and they'll have prints now. I want you to bring them here and compare them with Simon's. Some are sure to fit. I want to know about any others you find."

"Will you be here?" asked the jolly-faced Gildersleeve. "Or shall I go ahead an' wake him for the prints?"

"I'll be here till you get back. I don't want him left alone a single instant," said Masters. "The windows of his chamber and bath are all locked, unless he's opened them."

"Not him!" grinned Gildersleeve. "And there wouldn't be any way to climb into the rooms, anyhow, except maybe letting down a rope from the roof. No heavy ivy on the walls, or drainpipes."

No sound came from the inner chamber, where Simon Corlaes slept. Masters dismissed Gildersleeve on the errand, then looked about him more closely at the living room of the suite. Here it was that Edward Green had been struck down, and here seemed to be the obvious place for his own headquarters.

It was a comfortable room, with four windows facing east. One huge Kermanshah rug came to within a yard or thereabouts of each wall; and its deep blends of Burgundy and claret were rich and restful. A wide hearth came between the two pairs of windows. The whole wall opposite was devoted to book shelves which reached to the ceiling.

The books inside the locked glass cases, however, were bound uniformly in hand-tooled Spanish leather, with titles in gilt. They did not look as though they ever had been read.

One long table with a lamp near each end, stood in the center of the room. An old-fashioned but extremely comfortable davenport was backed against one side of the table, facing the hearth.

Gayly upholstered cane and rattan armchairs stood about, with reading lamps near each. Smoking stands, a Stromberg-Carlson radio receiving set, and a curious rack like an oversize muffin stand, holding four complete hookah pipes and a bronze humidor of fragrant tobacco, completed the furnishings. There were no pictures, and only one stag head with antlers. This was synthetic, and possessed only the one doubtful virtue of not attracting moths.

Thankful at the opportunity to work for a short period before the household stirred and beginning to chafe at a tightening leash, Masters took the set of blueprints of the

manor house, and studied them until he was familiar with
the layout of rooms.

He knew the grounds reasonably well, since this was one
of the show places of Long Island.

Biskra Bay, an arm of the Sound, came south a considerable distance from the line of Great Neck and Roslyn. The
Corlaes estate, not in the strict sense a manor, surrounded
the southernmost bend of the bay. From this the land
extended south to Highway 25A, the northern branch of
the Sunrise Highway.

East and west the land extended roughly two miles. On
each extremity were two tenant farms, all four small in area.

The rolling hills directly back of the manor house were
heavily wooded. The servants' lodge was concealed there;
and the whirring of partridge and quail coveys greeted a
visitor who trespassed on foot.

Simon allowed no hunting, as he had a fear of guns—
even those loaded with dust shot.

Along the bay was a wide yellow beach, the sand for
which had been brought in trucks from out near the Islips,
on the other side of the island.

Above this were two terraces, landscaped formally. Then
the great manor house, semi-Tudor, shaped like an I-beam
or a dumbbell, with eight turrets on the extremities of the I.

Just above the beach, half a mile from the manor house
bathing pier, stood a concrete building with small windows.
A high wire fence surrounded it. This was the laboratory
for chemical experimentation. Simon Corlaes had another
inside the manor house itself, a room which adjoined his
living room and bath; but the latter was not open to his
assistants, save on invitation. Here he pottered around,

using queer, expensive gases like argon, krypton, neon. Henry Handley Oliver merely shrugged and smiled when anyone asked what went on in there. The employer was keen enough for practical results in his big laboratory, but in his own workshop impractical dreams probably held sway most of the time.

LIEUTENANT CONNOR, LOOKING harried, came up to the suite at that moment. Masters saw that he was impatient to begin questioning Simon Corlaes, but it was not yet seven o'clock. Of course the millionaire did not have to be coddled, yet Masters felt sure that a quizzing of a man in the state of nervous collapse in which Simon last had appeared, would be less productive than such a questioning given, say, at eight or nine o'clock.

"I questioned him before bringing him back here," Masters reminded the lieutenant. "Unless he is the murderer, which I admit is a possibility, he knows too much—and too little. We will have to put on the screws, and make him tell a whole lot he'd rather keep secret."

"Damn his feelings!" snorted Connor.

The ruddy-faced assistant, Gildersleeve, came back then with damp but readable photographic evidence concerning the fingerprints left on the warning letter received by Simon Corlaes.

"They're all the same, made by somebody who was sweatin' like an ice pitcher," grinned Gildersleeve.

Masters examined the photographed smudges carefully under the light for a moment, then nodded. "Undoubtedly those of Simon Corlaes, though we'll check to make sure," he said. "By the way, Connor, the typing of that note of warning—it was done on an Underwood No. 5, I believe.

Is there such a machine around this house? Look for one that hasn't been hammered much. The note was all in capitals. You'll have them examined for peculiarities, of course."

The lieutenant pencilled a note in his pocket memorandum book.

"We haven't searched any of the rooms, so I don't know about the typewriter," he said. "Not likely a killer would come to his victim's house to do his correspondence, though. What I'm anxious about, is to get to examining that man in there. He—"

As if in answer, there came from the bathroom, adjoining the living room of the suite, a steady, faint sound of running water.

"Takin' a bawth now," said Gildersleeve broadly. "He's got a tub as big as a small swimmin' pool, one of these cabinets where you snap on hot lamps an' just sit an' sweat, an' an electric bath where you get jiggly little shocks all the time, an' a fancy cabinet they call a rose shower, where the water hits you all ways to once."

"Well, that's the shower, running now," said Connor. "We'll wait ten minutes, then give him the works."

Mild-mannered Barnes came in, bringing back the gray sock which he had taken to Masters' own small laboratory for examination. He drew his chief aside, speaking to him for two or three minutes, and giving him the wrapped sock.

Masters tore off the paper, and turned to the policeman.

"We know a little more about the owner of this death weapon now," he said quietly. "He is probably about six feet in height, young, athletic, and hard up for money."

He held the sock up.

"Wha-at?" cried Connor, staring at the grotesquely

shaped and tiny sock. "A six foot man wear *that?* And—"
He looked with suspicion at Masters; for Selwyn Connor
remembered other occasions on which strange statements
from the private detective had been found to be accurate.

"The darning shows that the owner was not given to
wasting money," said the detective. "Socks like these,
bought probably a couple of years ago, cost from five to
eight dollars a pair. The man who owned these took care
of them, probably because he couldn't afford any more
imported ones.

"Then something happened. Probably they acciden-
tally got into the laundry which was sent out—you know,
woolen socks like these have to be washed by hand, and
carefully, or they shrink. These shrank, and were no use
thereafter. I had the fabric examined under a low-power
microscope, and the original size of the socks estimated.
They were size 11½. That goes with a 9½ or 10 shoe. A foot
that size goes normally with a man six feet tall, though of
course there are exceptions both ways."

"Huh, mine are twelves!" said Gildersleeve. "An' I'm
only five—"

His sentence was broken off in a startling manner. It
seemed that for the fraction of a second, the water in the
running shower bath ceased to flow. Then it began with a
louder, almost thunderous sound!

And, simultaneously, there arose from within the bathroom horrible, rending screeches of terror and agony, the
high-pitched shrieks of a man in death extremity!

Then, within four seconds of time, before any of the
men in the suite living room could move a muscle from

the petrified surprise that gripped them, the noise stopped abruptly. Only the murmur of water remained.

"They got Corlaes!" cried Jigger Masters, leaping for the door. It was bolted securely from the inside.

5

DEATH IN A BATH

THE DOOR FROM the living room to the bed chamber of Simon Corlaes' suite was of two-inch quarter-sawed oak, set in a steel frame finished to simulate wood. One man, or a dozen at once, would fail to smash it or the chilled steel bolt which held it closed.

"No way into the bathroom from the corridor?" questioned Jigger Masters, turning. His face had gone pale with dread of what he would find behind that locked door. He, Masters, had been employed to safeguard the life of Simon Corlaes!

"Mebbe he ain't dead!" suggested Gildersleeve, Masters' assistant, huskily. He lifted the revolver he had drawn automatically and pounded on the oaken panels. There was no answer, even when he shouted.

"We've got to break in!" said Connor. "My God, there isn't any possible way—"

"Look out in the corridor, Barnes," Masters directed his other assistant. "I think I saw a fire hose and axe down at the end. If so, bring the axe. You, Connor, call up some of your police, and keep out the guests. Might find where each one comes from now, if you go out in the hall."

Though he left the spot even momentarily with obvi-

ous reluctance, Connor was too good an executive to omit
this precaution. A moment later they heard his voice, curt
to the guests who came in lounging robes from their various rooms, and crackling as he issued commands to the
uniformed men. He sent a patrol out to see that no one
left the house or grounds, then busied himself noting the
people of the house and whence they seemed to have come.

As far as he could determine hastily, they all had been
in the bedrooms assigned to them. Only one was fully
dressed. That was Stella Mallen, the hostess of the week-
end party that had begun so gruesomely.

Barnes came running with the fire axe. Gildersleeve
took it from him as a matter of course, and both came into
the living room at a run. Gildersleeve's short, heavy arms
lifted, and the axe fell upon one of the oaken panels with
a splintering crash.

Two more blows, and there was a hole through which
Masters thrust a long arm, finding the steel bolt and opening it. Together the three men dashed into the bedroom,
Barnes with a revolver, and Gildersleeve still holding the
axe.

The bedroom was empty. A pair of pyjamas lay rumpled
on the floor. The door to Simon's elaborate bath—a room
as large and even more luxuriously appointed than his
bedroom—stood open. And from it curled a thick cloud
of hot steam.

"Shut off the water if you know where it is," commanded
Masters. "Can't see a thing. Can you open a window,
Barnes?"

He also groped a way through the woolly blanket
of steam, until his hands encountered a tall glass cabi-

"He's in here, chief—dead. Say, I can't get out!"

net within which the water still was running full force. The water faucets were inside this, of course. Masters felt around the hot glass until he located the door.

It would not open!

"Quick! Up you go, Barnes!" directed Masters, motioning the little man to put a foot on his bent back and climb over the top of the glass cabinet which did not reach all the way to the ceiling. "Shut off the water and open the door. He has it on the latch some way inside—if he's in there at all!"

Masters was beginning to wonder, to feel just a trifle apprehensive. He could not see through the steam on the glass, and wondered if Simon merely had got under water too hot for him, and had fainted from the scalding. Certainly no one but a Japanese could bathe with comfort in water at such a temperature!

Of a sudden the water stopped. Then the voice of little Barnes:

"He's here, all right, Chief! And he's dead, I'm afraid. Say, I—*I can't get out!*"

The pause had come when he evidently had thrown his weight on the chromium lever which closed the lock of the door.

"Break this lock, Gil!" commanded Masters sharply. "Here it is." He guided the groping hand of his assistant. "And use the back of the axe."

Two blind smashes with the tool did for the lock. Masters yanked open the door. Out staggered the half-smothered Barnes, then stooped and pulled forth the inert body of Simon Corlaes.

"I didn't get a window open," Gildersleeve gasped. "They got fancy catches of some kind. Let's pull him into the other room. Is he dead?"

LIEUTENANT CONNOR, HIS work outside placed now in the hands of subordinates, came hurriedly to the steaming doorway. He was just in time to see Masters and Gildersleeve carry out the horridly red, naked body of Simon Corlaes, lifting it to the rumpled bed from which the man had risen only ten or twelve minutes earlier. Barnes, breathing with some difficulty from inhaling so much steam immediately after his climb, followed them, wiping water from his streaming face, head and clothes.

"Lordy, that was hot!" he muttered. Then in a louder voice, "Did it bump him? Danged if *I* could stand it any length of time!"

Masters made a speedy but thorough examination of the unlovely body. Then a baffled sound escaped his throat. He straightened up, face pale, and with grim lines etched from beside his nostrils to corners of his wide mouth.

"Dead, all right!" he admitted curtly, shaking his head at Connor's grave concern. "Send for Cortelyou. Oh, by the way. This may be shock—though I doubt it. If it is, an injection of adrenalin… see if that Dr. Herschel has come from Biskra Harbor. Someone sent for him, to tend Mr. Glendon."

But the amiable and easy-going Dr. Herschel had not yet come. He did not put in an appearance, as a matter of fact, until after eleven. Long before then, Simon Corlaes was stiff.

At this moment, though, the master of Corlaes Manor lay before a group of fascinated men.

"Not a scratch on him from head to foot," said Masters. "But look at these things—and the color of his skin, Connor. What do you make of it? Was he actually *boiled?*"

The things to which the detective was drawing attention were rows of huge blisters, white against the vivid scarlet of legs, chest, back and arms. They were extraordinary blisters, too, ranging in size from one grand-daddy of them all, a four-inch ovoid, down to strings of little ones about as big as dimes.

"Guess it was a scald, all right," agreed Connor. "He wouldn't have had much skin left, even if he had managed to get out of that cabinet. Hell of a thing to do—lock yourself in such a place!"

An exclamation came from Masters. Then:

"Take a look at that fastening we broke, Barnes," he commanded. "It will be very odd if there is a lock—on a rose shower!"

"No, there isn't, Chief," came the subordinate's answer a moment later from the still steamy room. "I guess we jammed it, though. It doesn't work now."

"Take it off. We'll examine it later."

There was nothing further to be done with the body, before the coming of either Dr. Herschel or the medical examiner.

Masters and Connor together went around the house to examine all the windows.

"They're all locked from the inside with these patent catches—every last one of 'em," said Connor at last. He looked sidewise. "I was standing outside the living room door every minute. No one came out. The living room windows are locked, as we know. Did you have any idea it might be—murder?"

Without replying, the detective strode back to Gildersleeve, touching him on the arm.

"Get hold of a thermometer, one that'll stand 212 degrees, Gil," he directed quietly. "Then go in and run that hot water from the rose bath tap. Find out just how hot it really is. Be sure that no one else is using it at the same time, so you'll get it as hot as it ever comes from the heater. And, by the way, it's probably an automatic gas heater. Make sure of that. Get the manufacturer's name and the model number."

WHEN GILDERSLEEVE HAD gone about this errand, Connor beckoned Masters back to the bed on which the body of Corlaes lay.

"I was just thinking of something that will ease your mind," said the policeman. "It will probably account for the funny color of the body—see, it's turning from red to purple now!"

"In spots!" agreed Masters grimly.

"Well, you heard about that devil-devil business, that speech Corlaes made when this party started?" Connor grimaced. "I wasn't here, but Corlaes is a chemistry magician, and this night he gave them some of his deep stuff. He appeared as a blue devil—a patron saint of the world depression, I suppose. Then he announced that prosperity was with us again. Pouf! went some steam. A chemical, of course. It changed him from a blue devil to a red one. You can see what that stuff was. There is some of it on a Turkish towel in the bathroom now. I'll bet that was what raised these blisters, and also what makes him this awful, color now!"

"Maybe it was poison, and killed him!" put in Barnes timidly.

Masters strode in, picking up the Turkish towel which Simon had used in scrubbing off the coloring matter from his hands. The detective took the violently blue-and-red towel out to the light, stared at it closely, sniffed it. Then he shook his head.

"Nothing but *lecanora tartarea*, with probably an extra dash of *orcein* for the deeper blue color. In other words," he explained to Connor, who was frowning, "nothing but an innocent vegetable dye-stuff allied to litmus. The acid he used to change the color to red smells like fairly strong acetic—the same stuff you get in vinegar. Under pressure it would heat, and then when released from a cylinder with a spray nozzle, it would come up like fog or steam.

There's nothing to account either for those blisters or for death itself."

He walked slowly back to the bed, and stood looking down at the bunchy, mottled body. Then he put down a spatulate forefinger, touching the queer blisters. These stood out firm in the skin; and below them the muscles showed gnarled and firm also, lacking any of the flabby collapse usually noticeable in a new corpse.

"Not much loss to Long Island-at-large," said Gildersleeve. "I reckon he was askin' for it, a long time."

It did not seem at all as if Masters heard. He had become suddenly rigid, bending lower over the bed. His hands passed over the arms and legs; and from a little distance Lieutenant Connor saw that the right arm, raised and then let fall, seemed to show a trace already of *rigor mortis!*

An inarticulate, savage sound came from Masters. Instantly Barnes and Gildersleeve were on the alert. They knew this sign in their chief, though what discovery Masters could have made at that time was hard to imagine.

He bent and lifted the body, placing it on its side.

At that moment there was a knock at the door, and Barnes opened it.

"The medical examiner," he said.

"Just a moment," said Masters, his resonant voice husky with excitement. "You, Barnes, Gildersleeve, Connor—this case has become a point of honor with me. This man was murdered."

"The hell you say!" breathed Gildersleeve.

"Now, before anything happens, before Cortelyou says anything that will astonish you, remember that I *insist* on none of you saying a word outside this room! Not until we know more!"

"Well, that's all right, I guess," said Connor, frowning nervously at thought of an inquest, and the barrage of reporters he would have to face soon. "Shall I let him in?"

CORTELYOU PUSHED IN as soon as Barnes released his hold. "What on earth's gone wrong with you men—and this confounded place?"

He caught sight of the naked corpse then, and even his professional irritability was banished. He crossed the rug swiftly to the bedside. "He looks like a decalcomania transfer!"

Quickly then Masters told him of how they had heard the dead man's shrieks, and the circumstances connected with finding and rescuing the body from a hot bath. The medico removed his gloves, and got down to work with a stethoscope.

"Dead, all right," he said in a moment, taking the stethoscope from his ears and laying it aside. "Hm, a hot bath… How long ago was that?"

"Twenty-seven minutes," said Masters, glancing at his wrist watch. "You made good time."

"I hadn't got to my second cup of coffee," the doctor said dryly. "Hm… what kind of a bath was he in? You said *hot!* But these blisters were never made by hot water!"

"Doctor," said Masters, "I haven't wanted to prejudice your mind, but will you do one thing more or less in advance of the autopsy? Right here, or any other place where it won't matter"—Masters indicated the heavy thigh—"make an incision? A deep one!"

Cortelyou dipped into his surgical bag, and brought

forth a small Weiss knife. Three downward strokes with the keen, tiny blade, and he looked up.

"Now what?"

"Put your finger down in that—*and leave it there!* That's right. Now, it may have been you had boiled eggs for breakfast. If so, when they had cooked four minutes or five, your maid probably took them out of the boiling water and held them in a spoon under the cold faucet a minute or so."

"Yes, what about it?" Cortelyou was shifting uneasily, and looking down at his half-buried finger.

"That cooled off the eggs so she could break them and fill your dish. But if she had let them stand just a few seconds longer, what would have happened?"

"They'd have got hot again!" snapped Cortelyou. "Sa-ay, can I take my finger out of here? It's—"

"Exactly!" said Masters in a tense voice. "Now tell me, doctor, from the feeling of your finger—you can take it out if you wish—isn't that body, which was immersed in a hot bath for a short time—*isn't it getting cold again?*"

"Hm! Hm! Why, ye-es, it is," responded the medico cautiously. "Now, just what on earth? Simon Corlaes must have had a normal body temperature before death of ninety-eight and six-tenths degrees Fahrenheit."

"Before death, yes!" snapped Masters. "Unbelievable as it sounds, doctor, I am suggesting to you that Simon Corlaes was murdered. That he was killed while under a shower of hot water. And that the agent which killed him was one which deprived his body, almost instantly, of every particle of human warmth!"

Cortelyou inhaled deeply. Then he bent and made a

second, more thorough examination. And as he did so, the frown on his forehead deepened. At last he straightened.

"I don't wish to sound too certain, before I perform the autopsy," he said, "but there is nothing I can see which runs counter to your suggestion, Mr. Masters. Except for the blisters, which just possibly might have been caused by very hot water, even after death, Mr. Corlaes might have died from exposure to cold. Certainly the quick rigor, and the chilliness of the tissues just below the fascia layer, make it look that way. I will bear in mind—"

"Bear in mind just this!" broke in Masters. "I suggest that Simon Corlaes was alive and in good health when he stepped into that rose bath and turned on the hot water. That he was killed there in the space of less than thirty seconds. And that in this short space of time his body *was literally frozen to death!*"

Amid a breathless silence on the part of the other four men, he turned on his heel and strode into the bathroom where Simon Corlaes had died.

6

MINUS 200° CENTIGRADE!

"WAIT!"

An astounded Lieutenant Connor hurried to the doorway through which the detective had vanished. Masters looked around, halting a moment.

"I won't be very long," he assured from between taut lips. "Send up your fingerprint men, though. Let them wait out there. Tell Gildersleeve and Barnes to be ready. I may want them to do something rather sudden."

"But these guests!" breathed Connor. "I've kept them in a huddle out there in the hall. Can't—"

"Suppose you have them all get back to their rooms and dress. Perhaps those who are hungry could have trays sent up from the kitchen. I'll want to start questioning soon now.

"Oh, yes, one more thing. You were inquiring about that man named Stanley Kershaw. I want him worse than ever now. He had something to do with an invention employing gas—something like this man Oliver had with another gas now used commercially. Only Kershaw didn't get any job or other satisfaction. I think he was simply robbed."

"I have a good man on his trail," said Connor. "We ought to hear any time now. Is there anything more?"

"No. Handle the guests and the people in the house as gently as you wish; but don't let any of them, or the servants, leave for any reason."

"All right. I'll send up the fingerprint squad."

The policeman took his leave, and Masters turned back into the bath. The air was still heavy with steam. His first act was to go to the windows, scrutinizing the fastenings of each. All were double-locked, patent spring catches at the sides supplementing the sash locks. It appeared certain that no intruder could have left the bathroom this way, even though an eighteen-inch ledge a foot below the window sill would have made progress from one room to another otherwise easy.

For one brief moment Masters looked from the windows. This bathroom, the bedroom, the living room and Corlaes' private laboratory took up the whole of the second floor rear, on this flange of the dumbbell. The windows were in plain view from the other rear wing, and also from a row of windows lighting a long corridor running the entire width of the second floor.

The air was clearing now, though the triple shatter-proof glass of the rose shower cabinet was still gray with condensed steam. Masters walked to it. The glass door hung open. The simple latch had been removed, and the glass surrounded this space with a sunburst of radiating cracks. Gildersleeve's blows with the axe.

With a dry Turkish towel the detective scrubbed away some of the moisture over an area of half the height of the door. Then he leaned close. He had found what he had reasoned must be there.

The triplex glass had not broken; but over the entire surface ran a network of fine cracks, like crows' feet.

These cracks showed not only on the door, but on the three immovable sides of the cabinet as well.

"Caused by the sudden change in temperature," grimly reflected Masters. "But how—and *where* did the freezing cold come from?"

He had more than half expected to find an apparatus of a strange sort inside the cabinet; but save for the shiny levers which adjusted the water to hot and cold, and the twenty or more spray nozzles which sent water upon the bather's body not only from above but from all sides, there was nothing at all inside.

He looked at each one of these needle-spray nozzles. Two of them, faintly warm still, seemed ordinary enough. Then the third one made him exclaim in astonishment and satisfaction. The chromium-plated pipe which conducted water to this nozzle was split for a length of two inches!

Overhead still another one of the pipes showed the same tell-tale splitting.

"Sent the cold through all the nozzles at once! Simply enveloped him! Good Lord, it's a wonder he could scream even once!" grimly thought the detective.

He emerged to the bedroom, where Gildersleeve, Barnes and two of the fingerprint men waited.

"I want to get into the laboratory. It adjoins the bathroom. Opens only into the corridor, I understand," said Masters. "Anyone know about the key?"

"Wouldn't it likely be in his pants—or mebbe on a key ring in his chiffonier drawer?" suggested Gildersleeve. "S'pose I look."

WHILE HE SEARCHED, Masters went back to scanning the architect's blueprints. Something he had not considered important—a long, narrow closet, windowless, set in the wall between the bathroom and the laboratory, and marked "Plumbing"—now looked like the crux of the situation.

Naturally there would have to be a regular battery of pipes there, since in the bathroom alone were three baths and a tub almost large enough for swimming; while it was likely that any laboratory would have sinks, vats and so forth, furnished with water from the same supply pipes, and draining into the same main.

"Got it, I bet!" exclaimed Gildersleeve, who had been rummaging in the small top drawers of a mahogany chiffonier. He held out a flat leather key case, unsnapping it and showing nine keys. "One of them, mebbe."

Masters nodded. "You two come along. You fingerprint men can wait here. I'll call for you in a few minutes, probably." He went from the bedroom through the living room, and thence to the corridor, which now was deserted except for a patrolman who sat in a chair tilted back against the wall. From his position he could see all these doors, the back stairway leading to the turret above and the first floor below, and the long corridor stretching westward the width of the house.

One of the keys fitted, and all three men entered the laboratory, a large, light room. Four windows occupied the west wall.

There was remarkably little apparatus in sight. Sinks and wash vats with fume hoods occupied the inner wall—next to the bathroom—as Masters had guessed. Opposite these was a long, low metal enamel cabinet built in, and looking as though its strength of design was intended to conceal formidable machinery.

An engraved German silver inset bore the words:

Hamson-Linde-Claude Cascade Liquefier.

"That's the thing!" said Masters from between gritted teeth. "Get the fingerprint men, Barnes, and have them go over all the outside metalwork. It's not much use, because you have to wear gloves in this business anyhow. But they can try. Don't let them open anything, though, if they value their fingers!"

"What'll it do to their fingers?" asked Gildersleeve wonderingly.

"That," Masters said slowly, "is the most efficient machine in the world for commercially producing low temperatures. When it is going, they get about 200 degrees below zero Centigrade, with no trouble at all. Probably lower than that in the latest models. This chills gases. They are liquid then, of course."

"Oh-h, liquid air!" said Gildersleeve. "That's the idea, Barnes, d'you see?"

They both turned to look at Masters, who was peering down at a three-foot door set between two of the soapstone sinks. Of a sudden Barnes recalled that he was to get the fingerprint men. He hurried out.

Masters crawled through the small door and out of sight. Gildersleeve bent down and peered in, obviously afraid that whatever it was that had killed Simon Corlaes might have enough punch left to account for a second victim.

"Don't take any chances, boss," he said.

Masters laughed grimly. "There's no danger here now,"

he said, flashing his electric pocket lamp on the uncov-
ered pipes.

A glint of metal on the floor attracted his eye. He bent,
and picked up a Yale key, one which looked to be very
similar to the ones found in the chiffonier. Handing this
to Gildersleeve, Masters directed that the latter try it on
the laboratory door.

"It works," said the stocky one succinctly, a moment
later as Masters crawled out of the wall door. The detective nodded, taking back the key and stowing it carefully
in his watch pocket.

The fingerprint men dusted the face of the enameled
cabinet, and the tops of two zinc tables laden with racks of
test tubes, Dewar flasks, Bunsen burners with their tubing,
filters, and other small apparatus.

"There's only a few prints, and they're old. They match up
with what were on that letter," said one of the men. "D'you
want pictures? And then, d'you want us to dust all them
bottles? We haven't touched 'em yet."

He indicated the top of the big cabinet, where in long
rows stood bottles and jars of reagents, each with its
black-lettered label stating the chemical contained.

"Never mind the bottles. Make pictures of those prints
you've found on the cabinet. Then, if no one has taken the
finger, thumb and palm prints of Simon Corlaes, you'd
better hike along to the morgue and get them. I'm not
interested in any prints, unless they *differ* from his!"

WHILE THEY SET their camera and made the exposures,
Jigger Masters sent Barnes for Connor. As soon as the way
was clear, the detective squatted down before the big doors,
four in number, which gave access to the cooling chamber,

the compressor machinery run by a small electric motor, the compression vat, and the refrigeration compartment for filled receptacles.

The first door opened easily enough, and with a quick glance before he closed it again, the detective saw that this was the compartment he wanted, the refrigeration vault for filled receptacles.

In the brief time the door was open, a terrific corroding chill had stolen out of the aperture. Twice as low in the Centigrade scale as the lowest temperature ever recorded in Nature (109 degrees *Fahrenheit* below zero, on top of Mt. McKinley) this avid finger of searing cold stole out into the laboratory and sucked many degrees of summer warmth from the room.

Lieutenant Selwyn Connor knocked on the door and was admitted.

"Just in time, Lieutenant," nodded Masters, stern satisfaction in his voice. "I am able to clear up a little of this confusion now. I propose to show you briefly how Simon Corlaes was murdered. The means is remarkable. I may say that it eliminates nine-tenths of the people who might otherwise be suspects."

"Thank the Lord for small mercies," said Connor. "Say, isn't it cold in here?" He looked about, and shivered slightly.

"It will be colder," Masters assured him grimly. Then turning to his stocky subordinate, he said, "You go around always with a pair of leather gloves in your pocket, don't you, Gil? All right, put them on now."

Masters explained that he wanted the first of two metal jugs to be lifted out of the refrigeration compartment, instantly when he opened the door. The jug should be set down until Connor viewed it and understood its purpose, then carried to the plumbing closet where Masters had found the Yale key.

"Work fast. And be sure not to touch any bare skin to that metal jug, or you'll be sorry!" the detective warned.

Gildersleeve got the double-walled metal flask with its flexible hose out in the room, and Masters gave Connor a brief description of the jug itself.

The container was in principle something like a thermos bottle. "The chances are that this contains some liquid air under high pressure," said Masters. "Now, bring the jug and hose into that closet, Gil. And you come along, Lieutenant. I want you to see how the murderer was able to shut off the water from that rose shower, and send in liquid air through all the spray faucets!"

The police officer watched then as Masters attached the flexible hose to the spout of the jug, then screwed it to an outlet on the hot water pipe which supplied the rose shower.

This outlet was used normally with a plain rubber hose, to bring additional hot water into the laboratory, when that was needed. A shut-off below the outlet made it simple to attach the flexible steel hose now.

"Normally the water would come out toward us," said Masters. "But with the water shut off, the pressure of the liquid air forces *that* liquid through, instead! The murderer shut off the cold water too, turning this little wheel on the other pipe. If he hadn't done that the pipes would have choked with icicles, and burst. Even as it was, they cracked.

"Now, you go in the bathroom, Connor. Gil, you and Barnes go too. I need you as witnesses. Close the door to the rose bath, and I'll turn on this cock, sending in liquid air for just five seconds. That will be enough. Stay away from the stuff as it comes, though. It's dangerous."

"All right. I'll rap on the wall when we're ready," said Connor.

The three took their departure.

A half minute later raps sounded. Masters bent, and opened the vent cock of the jug. The flexible hose leapt like a striking serpent, and there sounded a thunderous roar like that of live steam escaping from a safety valve.

Above this sounded a human cry of pain and surprise!

"Damn fool wouldn't believe me!" gritted Masters, and shut off the liquid air.

As quickly as possible he got to the bathroom. There he saw Connor, his face flushed with angry shame, tightly holding the fingers of his right hand.

"I don't want any sympathy, Jigger!" he snorted on seeing the detective. "I asked for it. The stuff looked just like water, so I put my hand there in the hole where the lock came from. Holy Moses!"

Masters took a swift, frowning glance at the dead white fingertips. "Hold them under the cold water," he directed. "That's as good as rubbing with ice. It will be lucky for you, though, if you pull a gun with that trigger finger again, Connor!"

7

HOSTESS ON TOAST

FIRST TO BE questioned, on the detective's list, was a man who might not be able to throw much light on the sequence of murders, but on whom Masters now had to depend, and to get in shape as quickly as possible. Lacey Glendon. Taking only Barnes, for the latter carried a stenographer's notebook and could write swift shorthand, Masters led the way out into the long east-and-west corridor.

Directly across from the apartment which had been occupied by Simon Corlaes, was the apartment of Mrs. Stella Mallen and her personal maid.

There were four guest chambers, two on each side of the main central staircase.

Next to the end apartment of Mrs. Mallen was a room previously occupied by Alicante, the dancer, and her middle-aged maid. Now Glendon had it, since he had been carried to the first chamber found open; and the dancer with her maid had been moved to a room the other side of the main staircase. Masters went to Glendon. And as he reached the door he came to a stop, frowning. The door stood ajar!

The detective breathed a deep sigh of relief when he ran in, finding Lacey Glendon in bed and breathing, though apparently still unconscious from his head bruise. The patrolman Connor had promised to leave there was not in evidence.

He muttered dark things about police in Nassau County. But the uniformed guard on duty at the head of the back stairway said that he had been in the room with Lacey Glendon. Then, at the alarm caused by the shrieks of Simon Corlaes, he had run, gun in hand, to that spot.

"You were right with Glendon up to then—and then what?" demanded Masters.

"I told the lieutenant that Glendon wasn't going to wake up for a long time, and asked if I couldn't do more good out here. I could listen for him, leaving the door open, and keep an eye on other things too. We were kinda short of men."

In spite of the fact that he sensed something uneasy in the policeman's manner, Masters shelved the matter for the time. Even if the uniformed guard was lying about something, Lacey Glendon was still in about the same condition he had been when carried up from the garage.

"Well, from now on I can't take any chances with Mr. Glendon," said Masters. "You or Gildersleeve will have to stay right in the room with him hereafter, Barnes."

"You mean—he might have been killed too?"

"Well, somebody tried once. And he ought to be a useful witness, if he saw anything at all, out there in the garage. I'm going to try to wake him now."

Glendon's pulse was still slow and uneven. Pulling up the eyelid revealed the fact that the man's iris was drawn half-upward. It seemed incredible that the small bruise on the forehead had caused such a condition, yet there was no gainsaying it.

Cold applications to the forehead and wrists did no more than make Glendon shift uneasily and mutter shapeless words. When they were removed he lapsed again into coma, though it seemed that his breathing was somewhat easier.

"It looks to me like this man ought to be in the hospital!" snapped Masters, deeply disappointed. "When the doctor manages to oblige us, and gets here, you ask him, Barnes, if Glendon doesn't need more attention than he's getting. A regular trained nurse, at least."

MASTERS LEFT THE room, closing the door. He searched out Connor, whom he found downstairs having a bandage wound around two fingers of his right hand.

Masters got the list of servants then, with their attached time-card statements. Each statement was signed.

"In about five minutes send Sorenson, the butler, up to me," said Masters. "About noon, suppose you have lunch on a tray with me up in Corlaes' living room. I should have something like a rough working hypothesis by then, at any rate. And I know you're under pressure from all sides."

"How about Glendon? He's about our best bet now, isn't he?" asked Connor.

"Still in dreamland. I wish Cortelyou had made another examination there. There are such things as cracked skulls, and Lacey Glendon bears all the earmarks of a deep-seated injury. I suppose now we might as well wait for the family doc, though." He went upstairs, glancing again at Glendon, and entered the room he now regarded as headquarters. Gildersleeve was lounging there, smoking his ripe meerschaum and looking pleased with himself. On the table before him was the chromium-plated latch which he had smashed from the glass cabinet of the rose shower.

"I took that thing apart to see what made it tick," he said, removing the pipe and gesturing toward the bath latch. "Somebody fixed it, all right!"

Masters reached out, but the subordinate caught his wrist.

"Just a minute, Chief," said Gildersleeve. "I've got that latch fixed just the way it was when old Corlaes went in to take his bath. Somebody intended that would be his last one, so balanced a little metal screw on the back of the spring plunger. Right inside there," he pointed. "Watch now. I can open the latch all the way, same like I was going into the bath cabinet. Then I can close the door, and everything will seem all right."

He suited action to his explanation.

"But now try to open it again! You can't! That little screw has fallen down in the way. It is just as good as a Yale lock!"

Masters nodded approval. "Good work, Gil," he said, and the ruddy-faced assistant flushed with pleasure. "There's no reasonable doubt that this murder was deeply and soundly planned."

"And the others were just happenstance?"

The detective shook his head. "Too early to say. Thus far it looks that way. If Glendon recovers, and can tell us who it was attacked him in the garage, we may have all this painful investigation short-circuited. Somehow I doubt that, though."

A knock sounded on the door.

"That will be Sorenson, the butler," Masters interrupted himself. "When you let him in, Gil, suppose you go and tell

Connor one thing. I'm interested now in knowing all about whether Corlaes left a will. Connor can learn the name of Corlaes' attorney. Better have him come out this evening."

Gil nodded. "And the lock?" he asked. "Shall I tell Connor about it?"

"Yes. Give it to him, and show him how it works. He'll need it as an exhibit at the inquest."

MASTERS GESTURED SORENSON in as Gildersleeve departed.

"Take a chair, Sorenson," said Masters, after a moment's scrutiny of the tall, middle-aged Scandinavian. The man bowed from the waist, and complied. Even when seated, however, his back remained straight. He had clear blue eyes, sparse, light hair of gray mixed with yellow, and straight, regular features. Probably a Continental-trained servant, surmised Masters.

This guess proved sound. Sorenson had been twelve years in America, and was a United States citizen. He had worked in Berlin before coming to this country. He had been in his present place five years; before that he had served in a Westchester family finally disrupted by divorce.

"You had your hands full, taking care of refreshments, most of the time?" asked the detective.

"Yes, sir, that is so," responded Sorenson precisely. "For the weekend all of us were to be busy every moment, as Mrs. Mallen had employed only two extra girls. Americans drink very quickly," he added, without the trace of a smile.

"Even Elsie, Mrs. Maben's maid, had to help," said Sorenson. "Poor Edward Green alone was upstairs. He had to wait until the master finished his speech, for then Mr. Corlaes would wish to bathe and dress in a hurry."

"All right. Now I want you to think carefully," said the detective. "Is there any one of the servants with a grudge? Did any one have cause to hate Mr. Corlaes?"

Sorenson shook his head with decision. "No, I am certain," he replied. "The work was hard, because since business became bad Mrs. Mallen kept only six house servants and a chauffeur—once there had been three chauffeurs, and twelve house servants. But Mr. Corlaes paid well."

"So you think that there was no chance that Edward Green could have cherished any hatred for Mr. Corlaes, for instance?" persisted Masters.

"No, sir. No one liked the master very much; but no one had any reason to hate him. No one of the servants, I mean, of course."

"Did Mr. Corlaes ever become violent? Did he ever strike one of the servants, to your knowledge?"

"Oh, no, sir!" A faint smile came for a moment into the butler's features. "Mr. Corlaes was—was not brave, sir. He did not like people even to talk about boxing and wrestling at table, for instance. I do not think he ever learned to fight with fists, like so many Americans do."

"I see," nodded Masters, who had formed about the same concept of Simon Corlaes' unlovely personality. "But you spoke of others, not servants, who had reason to hate Mr. Corlaes. Who were they?"

The butler stiffened. "I beg your pardon?" he almost stammered. "I am sure you must have misunderstood! I do not recall saying—"

"Hinted, then," snapped Masters, his manner suddenly changing. "It's no secret that Simon Corlaes had enemies.

I want your opinion about the people in the house. Who among those who stayed here, or who visited often, disliked him—or worse than disliked him?"

The butler took a deep breath. "All of them!" he breathed, seeming to collapse with that one effort, like a punctured tire. "But—but it is not my place to speak of such things. I—" He trailed off weakly.

A KEY GRATED in the lock of the outside door, and Masters started. He had not thought of anyone save Corlaes possessing a key, though of course Edward Green had, and probably one of the maids as well.

This was a tall blond woman, Stella Mallen. She came right in, frowning, and breathing as if she had climbed stairs rapidly. On the dead white of her cheeks two angry splotches of unshaded color showed like strawberry jam on a tablecloth. She wore a white linen dress and white sport shoes; but the ash-colored hair gave the impression of being done up hastily, and in the morning light lines that did not appear under the soft glow of lamps sharpened her features and made them vixenish.

"Here, too! And dragging out family scandals from a butler! Oh, this is unendurable!" she cried, balling her fists and coming towards Masters.

"You private snoopers! Get out, one and all of you! I simply won't have you in the house! Get out, I say!"

"I heard you. Sit down over there. Sorenson, you may go, for now," said Masters coldly. "Kindly do sit down, Mrs. Mallen."

Her head went back theatrically. Without a doubt the woman was angry, but she was yielding to it in a fashion which Masters would not tolerate. His hand, palm down, came with a thwack against the table top, and he rose to his feet.

He said icily, "I rarely sing for an audience, but I am going to ask you to listen to a few bars of song from an old, old show!"

Then, without preamble, his hazel eyes narrowed in menace and watchfulness, he sang:

> ... And some grand old reputations
> Would go off on long vacations—
> If a table at Rector's could talk!

The results exceeded his expectations, even though he had suspected she would flinch at being reminded of the Zeigfeld Follies of 1913, in which the song had been featured originally.

Stella Mallen stepped back, lifting the back of one hand to her mouth. The hectic roses drained from her cheeks, and the white-eyelashed eyes widened to unpleasing, pale-blue-centered saucers.

"You—you—" she choked. Then with a sudden gesture of weariness or hopelessness, she drew back the chair which Masters had previously indicated, and sank into it. "What do you want of me?" she asked dully. "I didn't kill anybody. All I wanted was to go in and see Lacey Glendon. He's hurt. He's a friend of mine. But oh, why aren't the police in charge?"

"They are," Masters assured her. "I was retained by your half-brother, Simon. Lieutenant Connor asked me to stay on and help him with the investigation. The three murders and an assault rather strain the abilities and personnel of a village police department."

He continued to watch her closely. He had suspected that she did not tell the members of her set that she once had been a show girl—in plain words, a chorus girl—but there was nothing really to be ashamed of in it that he could see. Stella Mallen either must take her half-doubtful position in this rather brassy, gold-plated society with intense seriousness, or else there was something more back in those pre-war years of which she was even more afraid.

"Now suppose you tell me your version of this affair," he bade, maintaining the chilly, suspicious demeanor which he saw had wilted her and made her apprehensive—of something.

"Ask the policeman. Connor, is that his name?" she flashed, with a momentary scowl. "I told him all I'd been doing. And believe me, if you think when you're running one of these week-end parties you've got time enough left to lurk around and murder valets—or even half-brothers who happen to need it—you've got a lot to learn, Mr. Detective!"

"WELL, TELL ME more," he bade urbanely. "You weren't quite frank with Lieutenant Connor, you know."

Masters knew nothing of the sort; but it was a safe statement with any important witness. He had never yet encountered one who was willing to talk without reservations, until forced. Those who babbled freely usually lied.

"I wasn't! Well, what of it?" she retorted. "I'll say this much more. All this good clean fun we're having is a family affair. First of all, I want to get that dancer and her maid, and Mrs. Gunter with her fool daughter, out of here. I simply don't want them around my house!"

"Hm. You call it your house," meditated Masters grimly. "That means, I suppose, that you have some knowledge of the provisions of Simon's will. Do you mean to imply that he left the manor to you?"

"No, I don't," she said flatly, the sullenness returning. "His will is right up there." She pointed at the top two rows of dummy books in the case. "Why don't you Jimmy-Valentine it, and let other people ask you questions, for a change?"

"We've sent for Mr. Corlaes' lawyer," said Jigger.

"Oh, old Jellybean Binney?" She shrugged. *"He* doesn't know anything. Cackled all over the place that Simon had drawn his own will, and not told even the witnesses any of the provisions! What a lawyer!"

"Well, do *you* know?" Masters' tone was still icy.

"I do not—except Simon once told us anybody who wanted to burgle that wall safe could find out. Only he or she would get a most unpleasant shock, probably. *I* think Simon's money will go to that little chit of a Gunter girl."

"There was some talk of an engagement between Miss Gunter and Simon Corlaes?"

"Yes. They had been engaged nearly a year, though it was not announced. I think Simon was getting over it. I know the girl was. But what is the use of all this? You know who killed Simon, and probably the other two men, don't you?"

"I'll be glad if you'll tell me just that little thing, Mrs. Mallen!" said Jigger grimly.

"All right—Marshall Corlaes!" declared the woman with sudden, unmistakable venom. "Simon's adopted son! His heir, if their fight didn't make all my precious half-brother's plans come unstuck. Oh, yes, you'll hear about the fight. Simon was in bed two weeks afterward—and he'd have been killed right then if Edward Green hadn't interfered."

"The valet! When did all this occur?" exclaimed Masters. He was aware that this woman was speaking from black and possibly unreasoning hatred; yet her words had the ring of conviction and truth.

"Months and months ago. Marshall got out of the house then, refused to accept an allowance any longer, *and never once entered the house again until last night!*"

"H-m." Masters considered rapidly. "You did not see him, then?"

"I didn't say that," she snapped. "He came to the grounds three or four times, I think, but always when I told him Simon was away. He came last night without being invited—and I myself saw him coming down from the house about twelve o'clock, a little while after Edward Green was killed, according to what my maid says! Green was the one who interfered the time Marshall struck down Simon, you recall!"

A knock sounded at the door. Masters glanced impatiently.

"I think I'll let you go for the moment, then, Mrs. Mallen," said he, rising. "Oh, just one thing. You're sure you don't know the combination of that wall safe hidden up there?"

"No. Nobody but Simon knew it, I'm sure."

"Well, anyway, you can show me how the book shelves swing out. Is there a button to press?" Masters brought a short ladder from the far side of the cases, pushing it on casters to the point the woman briefly indicated.

"Just twist that brass knob on the left-hand side of the second tier," she directed. "The whole half of two shelves swings out."

The knock on the door was repeated, but Jigger Masters ignored it. Following Mrs. Mallen's directions, he swung back the two shelves of dummy books, revealing a recess where the small but exceptionally strong wall safe lay.

An exclamation burst from the lips of Stella Mallen. Masters turned and looked at her grimly. Was this a real surprise to the woman? She looked as though the exasperating and strange discovery came to her as a great relief! She was almost smiling.

"Well," snapped Masters, slamming the shelves back in position, "the safe door stands wide open. And there isn't any will, or as much as a scrap of paper in it!"

"I think I'll have to congratulate Marshall, after all," she smiled. "He did *one* good job, anyway!"

8

GLENDON ACCUSES

THE NEWCOMER AT the door was Gildersleeve. Stella Mallen's chin swept up, and she passed out the door.

The stocky assistant grinned. "I had to help Barnes put her out of Glendon's room. She was goin' to go right in and nurse him, whether he needed it or not. Did she demand my scalp?"

"Not especially. I sang her a song," said Masters.

"You—huh?" Gildersleeve stared, then chuckled. "You sing about like you snore—which is praisin' with faint damns. Did she like it?"

"No-o. It reminded her of the time she was a Follies girl. Vintage of 1913."

Gildersleeve whistled. "Her!" he breathed. "Well, I'm glad I didn't get interested in anatomy till after the war. Florenz was some better as a picker, then."

"I rather like that woman," admitted Masters. "But you had something on your mind, Gil?"

"That fella Glendon. Doc Herschel's come at last, an' he's waked up our sleepin' beauty—some. Glendon thinks he knows who sloughed him, but—"

"But what? Whom does he name?"

"Oh, you go ask him, Chief," drawled Gildersleeve. "Says

I, he's either still dopey or lyin'. See if you think the same. Mebbe he'll have another idea by now."

Masters walked across the hall. Glendon's door stood open, and a mutter of men's voices sounded from within.

Barnes was seated inconspicuously in a leather chair set in the bay of one of the windows. Lacey Glendon, attired now in pyjamas, slippers, and a black silk lounging robe with silver stripes, was sitting hunched over on the edge of the bed. A pink, chubby young man with pince-nez, long black coat and gray-striped trousers, sat in a chair facing him. This was Dr. Herschel from Biskra Harbor, family physician to the very wealthy.

Dr. Herschel pressed the detective's hand three times, quite as if it were a fraternity grip, then dropped it suddenly.

"The great Jigger Masters," he breathed. "I have often read of your exploits. And to think I should be called in a case where you actually are in charge! My, my!"

"How's the patient?" asked Jigger brusquely, prepared to dislike the doctor most heartily.

"Groggy," croaked Lacey Glendon, looking up with a washed-out, one-sided smile. "If I try to stand I get seasick. Room goes round. Nasty bumps I got, but I'll be all right, give me a little more time. Any law against a good stiff snifter, Doctor?"

"No-o, I don't think so. Limit yourself to one glass of liquor, now, however. You are not in very good shape, you know."

He reached in his small satchel and brought forth a small bottle filled with a brown liquid, and labeled "French Brandy." He poured about two of the six ounces into the bottom of a tumbler which stood empty on the desk, and handed the glass to Glendon. He corked the little bottle and was putting it back when Glendon calmly reached over and took it, uncorking it again and dumping the rest of the contents into the tumbler. Then in two throws at his throat, he emptied the glass, making not even a grimace at the fiery liquid.

"Well, that's some better. So you are Jigger Masters, eh?" Glendon surveyed the detective with cool insolence. "I told one of your men, Gildersleeve, all I know. Oh, yes, and this chap Barnes was here. The three of you work together, I take it?"

"Yes," nodded Masters, not troubling to explain that Barnes and Gildersleeve were useful cogs rather than associates. "But if I can ask a few questions, and get your information down in the form of a voluntary statement, it will help a lot. Barnes, here, can take it as we talk. You don't mind, Dr. Herschel?"

"Oh, no; no indeed. You, Mr. Glendon," he said, snapping his satchel in preparation for leaving, "ought to lie around and take it easy. Stay in bed, or at least in any easy chair, two or three days. You'll be all right as soon as the dizziness leaves, I think. Avoid excess—of any kind."

"Thanks," grinned Glendon sourly. "It would be a blow to have to reform at my age. But you mean well, doctor. 'Bye."

MASTERS NODDED TO Barnes, and the latter took out a notebook and pencil. The little fellow had a faculty of making himself so inconspicuous that after the first moment or so very few witnesses recalled that he was there at all, taking down their every word.

Masters made his first queries commonplace. He learned

that Lacey Glendon was thirty-four years of age, a nephew of the deceased Simon Corlaes, and lived in a room at the Biskra Harbor Country Club during the summer months. Winters he spent in town.

"And your occupation, Mr. Glendon?" asked Masters.

The convalescent shook his head, then immediately caught it with both hands. "Ow-w!" he complained. "Don't crack any more funny ones like that. I forgot." He looked up, slightly cross-eyed, but then apparently regaining his equilibrium.

"The last thing I did was sell Insull Utilities," he went on then. "That's finished my career, depression or no depression. You see, I was innocent enough, but I stuck all my friends. They all cross their fingers and let the mastiffs loose now when I come around."

Without pressing the man to reveal exactly how he did manage to exist, Masters learned enough to know that Lacey Glendon probably had sponged upon Simon Corlaes and upon various friends and acquaintances, making the depression an excuse for loans, and for running up trades-man's bills which never would be paid. It was an old story to Jigger Masters.

"Now tell me," he said at last, "just why did you decide to go to the garage at that time last evening—this morning? Hadn't the police told you as well as everyone to stay?"

Glendon shrugged. "Oh, hell yes," he answered. "But I didn't kill old Green—liked him, the little I knew of him, in fact. So why should I drag along here, without any interest in the affair? I just slipped out to get my old bus. If anybody wanted to ask me questions, they could come and ask, couldn't they?"

"You kept your car in the house garage?"

"Oh, yes. I was over here a good deal. Habit to put it there, I reckon."

"Were you intending to stay for the week-end?"

"I hadn't been asked," returned Glendon flippantly. "Simon had taken $25,000 worth of those Chicago utilities—the ones that became worthless first—and he liked me about as much as he'd have liked a boil on the end of his nose. I got along all right with Stella, but not with him."

"I see. Well, on the way to the garage, did you notice anything out of the way? Was the garage lighted up? Suppose you tell it in your own words."

Glendon passed a hand over his forehead. "Well," he considered, frowning a little, "all of that's a little hazy to me now. I wouldn't care to sign any statement." He glanced momentarily at Barnes in the window. "What I think I know is so vague I wouldn't want it to be used as actual evidence in court. But I don't mind telling you, just as man to man."

"GO ON," BADE Masters.

"Well, I was hit *twice!*" was Glendon's surprising revelation. "But I'd better go back a second or two. The very minute I heard Lieutenant Connor telling the folks that a man had been killed up to the house, I faded out, went up to the kitchen entrance in the rear, and listened there. The door was open. I heard some man—the fellow who tends the fires, I think—"

"Walker?" prompted Masters.

"Yes, Walker. I heard him talking excitedly about how the police had been in taking care of the body of Edward

Green. I heard enough so I knew it wasn't any of my affair. I turned back towards the garage.

"Funny you should ask me about the garage being lighted. I noticed that it wasn't, and just sort of sneered to myself. Simon, you know, had instituted a whole lot of two-for-a-cent economies—like firing his two married chauffeurs, and keeping Haines, a bachelor, who would take less money. I thought Simon probably had issued orders not to waste electric light, even though Haines had to be on duty out there till the party was over for the evening.

"But I went right along in. Then it happened. I was just groping over towards my car. I remember I said, 'Haines?' sort of questioningly, wondering if he was there. I hoped he wasn't, of course.

"Between me and the door I got a momentary glimpse of a shadowy figure. Then something hit me on the top of the head and I went sprawling, pretty nearly out, I reckon."

"On the top of the head!" said Masters. "You're sure of that?"

Glendon grinned wryly. "I ought to be," he said, fingering the crown of his head. "There isn't any bump, but the whole top feels like it would come off, even now. Must have been a sandbag, like I hear was used on Haines."

"Who told you that?"

"Oh, Doc Herschel," said Glendon, and yawned. Masters from the corner of his eye saw an almost imperceptible nod of corroboration from Barnes.

"You say you had a glimpse of the man between you and the door. The garage doors were open, then?"

"All of 'em, I think. I know I didn't have to open any for my car."

"All right. Who was this man you saw at that time?"

"Well"—Glendon frowned with manifest reluctance—"he was tall, and he wasn't wearing a hat. A lock of his hair curled up in front, something like a cowlick. I saw that much in silhouette. And his arm was swinging. Then I went down. I hate to say it, for I've been pretty good friends with the man, but I'm morally certain it must have been H_2O—Henry Oliver!"

"He is the chief assistant here, I understand?" asked Masters, then went on before Glendon could reply. "What reason could he have for wanting to strike you down, or—kill you?"

"If he'd just killed Haines, and thought I was interfering with his getaway—"

"I mean personal reasons," said Masters. "The other probably is the explanation, if it was Oliver. But I want a line on your personal relations with him. Had you quarreled?"

"Oh—frequently! He's a redhead, you know," smiled Glendon. "But never seriously. There wasn't any reason. He's a good fellow. And no matter if he really was a sort of servant here, I liked him better than a lot of the half-wits who came as guests. Of course—" He hesitated, bit his lip.

"A girl, perhaps?" prompted Masters.

"Hmph," disparaged Glendon. "You'll hear about that, of course, so I may as well tell you there's nothing in it. H_2O was mad about a certain young lady, and I'd played around a little now and then with her. Nothing serious. As a matter of fact I happen to know that the girl was supposed to be engaged to another man—neither H_2O nor myself! But I think she really loves Oliver."

"And her name?"

"Huh. You're supposed to be a detective. You can find that much out for yourself. I don't care to be quoted in regard to any girl."

"Very decent of you, I'm sure," agreed Masters dryly. "Then this fellow you think may have been Oliver struck you a second time? How do you know?"

"Rats! I said nothing of the kind!" snorted Glendon, jerking up his head, and then suddenly clasping it, as an agonized expression swept across his features. "Ow-w, I forgot. What a head. Oh, suppose I tell you right straight through. I'll be ready to lie down a while then. I'm dizzy."

Masters said nothing, watching him as he took a deep breath and seemed to conquer the sensation.

"As I said, I went down to the floor," continued Glendon after a pause. "I wasn't clean out—not blankly unconscious, I mean. I think I was just pretty badly jarred and dazed, feeling as though the roof had fallen on my head. I remember grabbing out with my hands on the concrete floor, getting a handful of grease…

"Well, I opened my eyes, closed 'em again, and tried to struggle up. Probably I groaned, because I know I was sick clear down to my toes. I had got up as far as my hands and knees, I think. Then a man came running. Another man. He was sort of whimpering like a sick puppy. He crouched, yanked back his fist, and started a sort of an uppercut. That's what did knock me out completely, I reckon."

Masters' level eyes did not change expression. "But you saw this man more clearly?" he asked. "Who was he?"

"Yes, I saw him," admitted Glendon. "He was just a shadow, of course; but there's nobody else around this neck of the woods who ever walked with short, springy steps like that—or who had that bunchy, gnomelike figure. Since Al Corlaes killed himself, anyhow.

"No, sir! I don't know what to make of it, any more than I know why H_2O would want to wallop me in the first place—unless they were looking for each other, and both found *me* by mistake."

"And the second man was?" demanded Masters.

"The second man was Simon Corlaes himself!"

9

HOVERING MENACE

JIGGER MASTERS TOOK a turn out around the well-kept grounds before lunch. The day was warm. It would be pleasant down in one of those summer houses on the Sound.

Jigger descended to the lower terrace, and leisurely descended the flight of steps which led down to the yellow sand beach.

It was high tide. Even when he went out as far as the water's edge and looked back, he could see only the short cliff leading up to the first terrace. He was walking eastward on the sand, drinking in the sunlight and the warm summer air, deliberately putting aside all thoughts of the case, when he saw a man's figure. After a moment of scrutiny, he guessed the tall, athletically built youth clad in silver-colored trousers and white shirt must be Marshall Corlaes. Masters had seen this young man once, only for a moment, but had retained a vaguely pleasant impression of gray-blue eyes that looked directly at him, and a pleasant though slightly troubled smile.

Marshall Corlaes saw Masters, and came towards him.

"You are Mr. Masters? I'm called Marshall Corlaes,"

greeted the newcomer in a courteous voice, extending his hand. Masters accepted the grip, and liked its firmness.

"Well? How did Connor happen to allow you to come outside?" questioned the detective. He was scanning the other's face, and saw half-hidden in it signs of genuine trouble of some description. This was the youth accused by Stella Mallen, the young man who had quarreled with old Simon and struck him down. In a short sizing-up Masters felt disposed to guess that whatever Marshall Corlaes had done to a man so much his elder must have been prompted by provocation.

"I didn't have any breakfast, so I ate an early lunch," explained Marshall. "Then, as I had made a discovery, I spoke to the policeman up in the hall, and then saw Lieutenant Connor. I showed him what I had found, and it seemed to disturb him. He was trying to get a phone connection, though, and told me to go out and find you.

"And, by the way before I forget, he said that he had to call back the District Attorney, and probably would be about a half-hour late lunching with you."

"I see. And what was your disturbing discovery?"

"This!" said Marshall laconically, lifting an object from his right trousers pocket, where there had been an odd-shaped bulge.

It was an hour-glass, identical in shape and size with the one discovered with the threatening message by Simon Corlaes.

MASTERS TOOK THE object, and seemed to scrutinize it—though he knew there would be no fingerprints worth recording. He waited. Just what interpretation Corlaes had put upon this discovery would be interesting. As far as the detective knew, no one save Connor and himself knew of the previous threat. But in that surmise he was wrong.

Deep inside, Masters felt a constriction. There was bitterness in all this case, for him. He had been employed to protect the life of a man, and he had failed. True, the preparations for that murder had been made long before, and time had been short for uncovering them. Yet the failure remained as a painful fact.

Now, was this a sign that the killer had not *finished* his job? Or—was this youth, already accused of Simon's murder, attempting in rather childish fashion to throw dust in the eyes of the law?

When Masters did not speak, the other shifted impatiently—or was it apprehensively?

"Someone left that in my room last night after I had gone to bed. And the room was locked—the door, anyhow," he ventured. "I found it on *top* of these trousers I had been wearing. I'd folded them and laid them on the window seat."

"H-m. Were the sand grains running when you picked it up?" asked Masters.

"No."

"Was there any message of any kind?"

"No. Nothing."

As if lost in thought, Masters led the way to the stairs, and sat down, holding the hour-glass in front of him.

"I understand," hesitatingly began Marshall, "that another one of this set was found beside Simon's body—or near it somewhere. I wondered—"

The hazel eyes flashed up to his countenance. "Just where did you hear that?" demanded Masters.

"Why—uh—" The young man looked blank a moment. "Oh, it was when we all came out into the hall. The time we heard Simon's screams. We'd been there some time, when Lieutenant Connor came out, and sent us all back to our rooms. But before he did that, he said something about finding an hour-glass near Simon's body, and did any of us know anything about such an antique.

"Of course Mrs. Mallen and I did. There was a set of six hour-glasses kept downstairs in a Buhl cabinet in the west drawing-room. An antique set—this is one of them." He pointed. "Used to belong to Charles Fox, I believe."

Masters nodded slowly. If what Marshall Corlaes had said was not strictly true, he was in possession of damning knowledge!

Motioning for the young man to follow, Masters climbed the steps to the first lawn terrace. From this point all of the manor house, save the western extremity which was hidden by intervening copper beeches, was in view.

"Your room—ah, on the second floor, next to the main stairway," said Masters. He looked thoughtfully up at the two oriel windows. Both were partly open, the leaded panes held outward by steel arms. "Now, how do you think that hour-glass got into your room?"

Marshall shrugged and smiled. "Isn't it evident?" he asked. "Whoever planned Corlaes Manor might have been thinking of a paradise for cat-burglars. Why, this is the room I used to have when I was living with Mr. Corlaes. If I was in a hurry to get down to swim, or for any other reason, I'd slip out one of those windows on to the ledge or coping, or whatever you call it. From there I could swing down to the main stairs. Or I could come back that way, times I didn't want to see members of the household. You can get into any room in the house that way, provided the windows are open!

"It looks to me as though someone went prowling last night, lifted my screen—none of the screens is locked—and dropped my little present. Then he pulled down the screen and faded away. I didn't hear him, anyhow."

"And do you expect someone to make an attempt on your life?" asked Masters. "You sense that somebody really feels you made a mistake that needs correcting."

Marshall stared. Then his grayish eyes twinkled, and he laughed shortly. "Not very seriously," he admitted. "I can think of a person or two in this outfit up here who might like to hear of my being boiled in oil—Stella, for instance—but as for anyone actually starting a fire under the pot for me, no! I'm too unimportant. I haven't even been in the house before last evening, for almost a year."

"YOU CHOSE AN unlucky time to start in again."

"Not at all! Quite the contrary," grinned this extraordinary youth calmly.

"Oh, yes, I can guess what you're thinking. You're saying right now: ah, my cocky young murderer, d'you really believe police and detectives are so stupid you can walk up and pull their noses? Aren't you, now?"

He had the audacity to grin at Masters.

"Not so far from it," admitted the detective. "You *have* been accused of the three murders, you know!"

"I expected it," returned Marshall. "At least I did expect somebody would want to grab me for the death of Edward Green. At the time I went to bed I thought Simon had done that himself, along with the killing of Haines and the crowning of Prince Glendon; but I thought he'd hired you to dump the deadwood on some poorer and more convenient person.

"In Simon's eyes I'd have been a most convenient one! In all his life of cheating, lying, corrupting girls and women, and betraying his best friends, I think I was the only man to give him a taste of what he really had coming. Yes, he was afraid of me; and he had reason. I had thought over killing him, more than once!"

"See here!" said Masters sharply. "Do you understand what you're saying to me?"

"Perfectly!" retorted Marshall. "Look me squarely in the eyes! There. Now, sir, I tell you on my honor I *didn't* have anything at all to do with any of those murders! You can take that or leave it. But I'm sure of myself; and I'm willing to make quite a bet right now, for a poor man, that you've written me off the books! Am I right?"

Masters had caught sight of Lieutenant Connor emerging from the front door of the manor house, and coming purposefully in the direction of the beach. He said, "I've got a little confab, and then lunch, scheduled, Corlaes. I'll tell you frankly I don't know now what that hour-glass means; but until I do know I'm assuming you are next in line to be murdered!"

"Wow!" said Marshall joyfully. "I won't be bored a bit, now. Particularly if—but say—" He broke off, coloring slightly, as if he had caught himself just in time before saying something he did not wish known. "Don't I rate a snickersnee or something to defend myself with, when this sandbagger comes prowling?"

"Sandbagger—you know *that* too!" scowled Masters. "By the way, do you own a pair of gray golf socks?"

"Socks?" echoed Marshall, looking puzzled. "Why, yes, I do—or did. Haven't worn 'em for a year. They shrank," he explained. "Why?"

"Never mind," rejoined the detective with a mirthless chuckle. "Suppose you run down and have a smoke on that pier while I eat lunch. I've got a whole lot to ask you, later, and it would grieve me to beat hell if you got—uh—boiled in oil, first!"

Then he turned to meet Connor, thinking to himself that Marshall Corlaes was a young man whom he would have to keep away from questioning by Connor.

"I'm given until tomorrow noon to make an arrest!" snapped Connor in greeting. "Then the D.A. himself will take over—and you and I will—"

From an upper window sounded scream upon scream, in the voice of a woman! Then hoarse, questioning shouts!

"Bet some damn fool took a bath!" burst out Connor, and sprinted as fast as his fifty-six years would let him.

10

CARMINE DEATH

AS MASTERS AND the lieutenant reached the front stairs, another figure, running lightly but faster, joined and passed them.

"It's the girl—the dancer!" flung back Marshall Corlaes in a voice of horror. He swung open the heavy door, and darted through and up the main staircase. The two other men were on his heels.

The crowd in the corridor indeed was gathered about the door of the room now occupied by Alicante, the dancer, and her maid. This, Masters recalled, was not the room these two first had used. Mrs. Mallen had put them originally in the chamber now given over to Lacey Glendon. In carrying the latter upstairs, the police had taken him into the first room they found open. The dancer and her maid, therefore, had moved to the first chamber on the other side of the main stairway.

Both could be reached easily from the outside stairway, Masters realized in a flash. And both had been in the focus of this mysterious killer's renewed activities!

Two policemen were in the room, and a third stood at the door, keeping out the frantic guests. As Masters and Connor came shoving their way through, Connor spoke briefly to the uniformed man. The latter seized Marshall Corlaes by the elbows, and hurled him without ceremony back into the arms of a faded, austere woman Masters recognized as Mrs. Penrhyn Gunter.

"Nobody but police gets in!" he warned gruffly.

Not more than forty-five seconds had elapsed from the moment of those first screams before Masters and Connor were inside the room with the door closed. The police guards had acted with commendable speed; but they, like everyone else in the house, had been on their toes, fearful of something more to come. Their state of mind now was close to panic.

The dark-eyed dancer, eyes wide with fright and horror, stood between one of the twin beds and the window opposite its foot. A policeman, who showed that he had dragged her away, was watching her, and darting quick, apprehensive glances at the bed.

A second uniformed guard was at the bed, whereon lay a middle-aged woman. Her eyes were partly open, and the mouth was drawn in a tense, hideous grin, with spots of foam at the corners. The policeman, one arm under the rigid shoulders, had been trying to get the woman to drink a glass of water; but the uselessness of it was attested by twin streams which had run down the lipstick-reddened lips and the chin.

"Got a fit, I guess," the policeman muttered, glad to relinquish his task. "Found her on the floor. She was all stiff, and sorta jerking—"

Silently Masters made a swift examination. Then he straightened. "Take Miss Alicante out to another room," he

She could not summon the strength even to scream aloud.
This was one of the killers there in her bathroom!

bade in a sympathetic voice. "And phone Cortelyou. There
is nothing to be done for this poor woman."

"Oh-h, *Mumsy!*" cried the dancing girl, heartbroken.
She tried to come forward, and might have fallen had not
the policeman near her reached out an arm and steadied
her. "Oh, no, I won't go! Don't you understand? She's my
mother!"

There was no mistaking the genuine anguish. Masters
who, in spite of the professional dancer's beauty, had been
ready to put her aside as a mere employer of the dead
woman, instantly revised many half-formed concepts. A
dancer who brought her own mother along as maid and
chaperon! Well, the girl probably was not as hard-boiled,

then, as her usual sort. Certainly she looked young and stricken to the heart at this tragic moment.

Masters treated her with sympathy. He could not bring himself to banish her, so finally induced her to take a chair in the bay of one of the oriel windows, and drew a screen between that and the gruesome sight on the bed.

"I am horribly sorry, Miss Alicante," he said in a hushed voice. "There is no doubt that someone killed your mother, and I mean to find out who did it. Any time you wish I will have another room put at your disposal."

Words were of little avail, as he knew, but there was a comforting quality of grave strength in the detective's voice which seemed to help her to relax.

The terrified light in her dark eyes was replaced by a wistful sadness, and the tears came.

"Oh, Mumsy, Mumsy!" she sobbed, suddenly leaning her face into the bend of her arm, against the back of the chair. "Why should *any*body hate you?"

Jigger Masters waited a moment, then tiptoed silently back to the figure on the bed. His face was stern as he bent over, making a more careful examination of the face. Connor, looking old and haggard, stood by.

"It seems so senseless—all of it!" he muttered. "I don't suppose there is any doubt that this is murder, too?"

"None!"

MASTERS STRAIGHTENED, THEN bent again quickly, sniffing at the carmined lips of the dead woman. Then he walked away from the bed, and swooped on some object lying atop the small dressing table. He sniffed at this, and nodded slowly. As if forced to a measure he did not like, he returned to the girl seated there beyond the screen. Apparently she had not moved. Sobs of quiet despair shook her shoulders.

"Miss Alicante!" he said, touching her hand.

Slowly she roused herself, touched her dark eyes with a handkerchief, and looked up at him. He thought to himself that even in the pallor of grief she needed no cosmetics— and that this fact probably had saved her life! Wistfully beautiful, she would have stirred a man far more heartless than Masters. But he realized that just then she saw him only vaguely; that her every thought had gone in hopeless longing to the dead woman on the bed. He waited, silent, until she had quelled the outward signs of her emotion. Then she spoke.

"Our name is Graham," she said. "Mine is Dorothy. My mother is—was—Mrs. George Cantrell Graham."

"Thank you, Miss Graham," said Masters quietly. "I know now the means employed to kill your mother, and it is a terrible thing. Did your mother often use rouge and lipstick?"

"What? Mother? N-no, only once in a while. She didn't have any of her own. You see, I always had make up in my box; and since her hair and skin were about the same color, she used mine the few times she had any occasion— But what connection has that? You don't mean the rouge pot—"

She straightened a little, then half-recoiled as Masters held the white porcelain pot so she could see.

"You don't mean—*that* did it?" she whispered.

"Yes, I believe so. Now, Miss Graham, I don't know much about women's cosmetics. I didn't find any ordinary lipstick there in the array on the dressing table. Is it usual to use this sort of material—rouge, I suppose—for both lips and cheeks?"

She nodded. "Sometimes that's so. It is with me, anyhow," she said. "Of course you always have them the same tint, and I carry three shades to suit different costumes, you understand. Just for ordinary day use, though, both mother and I use that jar for lips and cheeks. Except on days I'm feeling sick, I never use make-up off the stage. I—I don't need it." There was a wan smile after that, quickly fading.

Masters nodded solemnly. The murderer, then, had not intended to kill the elder woman, but this lovely girl. If a homicidal maniac were ruled out—and the detective felt there was too much motive present here; too much deep planning exhibited in the previous deaths, for a crazy man—then an attempt to slay this dancer ought to narrow down a field of possible killers still more.

"And did you use this yourself, when getting ready for your dancing last night?"

"No." She shook her head. "That was another shade, darker. Until mother took this out of the make-up box this noon—"

"Then you saw her?"

"Y-yes. It was only—a little while ago. Twenty minutes or so. She said she was so pale she—she—" Of a sudden the sobs returned, and Miss Graham bowed her head in her arm again.

"Then I must advise you," said Masters in a low tone, not for any ears but hers, "to omit rouge for a time. Also, you had better take any meals you want with one of my men, outside. There is a poisoner loose, and it seems that he intended to kill you, instead of your mother!"

"Oh—it was poison?" Her horror-filled eyes came up to stare at him.

"The worst and quickest known," said Masters grimly. "Hydrocyanic acid! Enough was put in this rouge pot so that even smelling it is dangerous. Your mother dabbed it rather thickly on her lips, with a little on her cheeks—"

"Oh, I remember. She remarked that there was a different perfume about it than she had ever noticed before. Bitter almonds! That's what it was. I can smell it now."

Masters nodded. "The smell permeates the whole room now. But in this dilution it is not dangerous. Only when some is taken into the mouth, it is breathed in great concentration or it gets into a cut in the skin.

"But now, Miss Graham, I have to ask you a question. I want to know whom you would accuse, if you had to accuse *some*body in this house—or among the guests who attended the party last night? Who would want to kill you? Who has reason to hate—or to fear you?"

The dancer frowned, biting her lip. "Oh, there should be no one, really," she sighed. "Mother and I never had been on Long Island before we took the train at the Penn Station to come out here yesterday morning. We never had met any of these people. Mrs. Mallen engaged us because she had heard of us from Mrs. Geraghty, of Philadelphia.

"Of course there might have been someone in that crowd of guests—and yet I simply cannot think of anyone at all who hates me, or who had the slightest cause to hate mother."

"Well, then, how about love?" asked Masters seriously. "You will have to pardon me, Miss Graham, for questions that sound impertinent. But wasn't there some young man—or old man, even—who had made overtures to you? Whom you had turned down, and who had taken it badly?"

"No one!" she denied firmly. "I was engaged—until two years ago. That was in Paris. He died. Since then no one at all."

"All right then, Miss Graham. At a time like this I don't want to put you through an inquisition; but I simply *must* know more. Your own life is in danger! Also that of another person in this house!"

"ANOTHER? OH, *WHO*?" she cried.

"He can be left out for the moment. Let's take one thing at a time," said Masters with a shake of the head. "You tell me that all these people are unknown to you—"

"*Were* unknown—completely so," she broke in, a faint grimace of distaste curving her full lips. "There—there were small complications which arose immediately." She was speaking slowly now, weighing her words. Masters thought she was embarrassed for some reason. "Oh, I feel almost certain that anything I could say would only befog matters further for you."

"You must let me be the judge of that," said Masters. "Well? What happened immediately you got here? Did Simon Corlaes become objectionable?"

Slow color suffused her cheeks. Her eyes rose to meet his searching gaze, however.

"I do not think this is relevant at all. But I am willing to tell you in confidence. Only, I don't feel that I can—unless—unless—oh, I'll have to ask someone, first. There is a person—"

She paused, shaking her head in confusion. Stage dancer

she certainly was, but Masters saw that she could not do much with the histrionics of deceit.

Now she rose abruptly to her feet. "Oh, Mr. Masters," she begged anxiously, "will you let me have a few minutes' talk with someone? Then I think—I hope I can tell you all I know."

"Who is that person?"

"Marshall Corlaes!"

For the space of one heartbeat Masters was motionless. Then the beginning of a grim smile tugged at the corners of his wide mouth. The two latest-indicated victims of the manor house murderer were acquainted with each other, in spite of Miss Dorothy Graham's newness to Long Island.

"And is Marshall Corlaes a new friend of yours here?" he inquired.

She shook her head. "I didn't intend you to think that," she said, avoiding his searching glance. "I have never met, or even spoken a word to Mr. Corlaes."

"Hm," rejoined Masters doubtfully. "Well, that ought not to be hard to arrange. When last seen, Mr. Corlaes was trying his best to elbow a way into this room. I imagine they have him in a strait-jacket out there in the hall. Will you come now, Miss Graham?"

His visage was sardonic as he led a way into the corridor. Out there young Corlaes had evidently seen the light before it had become necessary to manacle him, for he stood glowering against the opposite wall. But at sight of the dancer an expression of incredulous relief flooded his features. No one had seen fit to tell him or any of the other people outside just what had happened inside the chamber; and among the small, panic-stricken crowd everyone had assumed the worst.

"Take the rest of these people all to some room down-stairs where they can be guarded," Masters said to the lieu-tenant. "Tell them I hope there will be safety in numbers.

"And now you, young man," he added, taking Marshall's arm, "come along into your room. This young woman is going to confide in me—after she has asked your permis-sion to spill the beans. I warn you that in time we'll have the story anyhow; but if she is to be safe meanwhile, you'd both better see to it that I know all there is to know.

"Perhaps even that won't be enough. We've had four murders here, one assault, and one warning which has not yet come through. You two are labeled. Suppose you chat now to your hearts' content, and then call me in when you're ready.

"I understand you two have not met. So—Miss Graham, allow me to present Mr. Corlaes." He bowed them into the chamber, and closed the door.

Then he turned away, going back to wait for the reap-pearance of Dr. Cortelyou, and attempt to weave all these seemingly unrelated acts of violence into at least the rough outline of a sensible pattern.

"That girl was telling me the technical truth," he reflected sarcastically. "She never had *talked* to young Corlaes. I wonder when and *why*, then, she wrote him a letter?"

The detective, whose dalliance with women usually had come at times when he suspected them of too free a hand with the Paris green, scarcely realized that dark eyes could answer so much—even when they did not use the language of love.

11

TURMOIL

A BAD HOUR for Masters ensued. Dr. Cortelyou was vindictive when he arrived, and talked continuously in a low, savage monotone concerning the inefficiency of police and detectives generally—with pointed references to the group of low-grade IQ's infesting Nassau County at the present time. The medical examiner had sufficient justice in his viewpoint so Masters left him abruptly. The detective was filled with a cold fury; yet senseless retorts to an irritated medico who had spent all his time since the first small hour of the morning on a continuous chase after or with cadavers from the manor house, could assuage nothing. This whole affair thus far was gruesome, bloody failure.

But not failure for the murderer or murderers!

"I feel as though we'd been wading in gore for a week," said the detective, drawing Connor away from the room in which the dead woman lay. "Let's see, it's just twelve hours since Mitsui woke me up to say Simon Corlaes wanted to see me!"

"Could you eat that lunch now?" asked Connor. "Me, I haven't a speck of appetite."

"No. But if they've got any of that beer left on tap, I could use a tall stein and a chunk of Swiss on rye."

Connor led the way downstairs, and after a grimace or two decided that he also could manage a sandwich and a drink.

They had this much refreshment standing, and during those few minutes a patrolman came to report that a newspaperman—or someone who claimed to be one—had been nabbed while climbing the fence to the estate.

"Hold him as a suspicious character," snapped Connor. Then, as the policeman swung away, concealing a broad grin:

"That's the third who's got in. I warned 'em! I've sent down two reports to keep 'em quiet. But, Lord! I hardly dare admit we've had another murder!"

"Many of them out there?"

"About twenty, last I heard. They tried to mob the gatekeeper, but he pulled a gun on them."

"Stout fella. Hm, I suppose you questioned him about this fellow Kershaw—the old partner of the Corlaes brothers?"

"Yeah." Connor sounded disgusted. "As far as I can make out, Kershaw—if he was here at all—didn't come in his own car, and didn't leave in anybody else's car. No cars left before the bunch I let go about half past one or quarter of two. Of course Kershaw was here. A half-dozen people saw him. But it's a long walk from the Mineola station, or from Roosevelt Field. Of course he could have got a cab."

"Maybe he has a boat?" questioned Masters.

"No, not unless it was a canoe. There weren't any motorboats. It was a still night, and the sound of one would have been heard, even when the orchestra was playing."

"But possibly not noticed. Have you searched through the shrubbery?"

"Ugg!" Connor choked on his beer. "My God, you mean—*another* body?"

But Masters was not speculating. "I want that man. He may know nothing at all; but there's no reason to think that the poisoned rouge was not planted at the same time Corlaes was done in. The killer could have dropped that hour glass—oh, I haven't told you about that, though I suppose you got a brief word from Marshall Corlaes?"

"Yes, he said something—I was busy. Sent him on to you."

"Well, take a deep breath. We've got to grab hold of this right now," said Masters, frowning slightly. "Our first duty is to see to it that there are no more murders! And I hate to say it, but I see no reason to think that the murderer was fooling at all, in the cases of young Corlaes and that dancing girl. The death of the mother was just an accident, possibly. Though he might have wanted to get rid of her, too."

"OH, I SUPPOSE I'm dumb. I don't see. I don't see anything," groaned Connor. "For instance—and I wanted to tell you and Gildersleeve before I forgot it—that door to the rose shower. The lock with the screw fixed to fall in it. You remember?"

"Rather."

"Well, it just wouldn't work at all!" The lieutenant shook his head disgustedly. "Look here. If that screw was in the lock, all poised so it would fall the next time the latch was opened and closed, old Corlaes would have been unable to close the door tight when he went in for his shower! Oh, yes, now wait, Jigger. He'd come up, twist the lever that opened the lock, swing the door open, *and then let go of the outside handle.* Of course he couldn't hold on to it, and close the door with himself inside. That would be too much, even for a contortionist like old Simon."

"You mean," broke in Masters, "that if things were as you've outlined, immediately he let go of the door handle, the screw would fall. Then the lock wouldn't open a second time, and the shower door could not be closed?"

"Yes, exactly." The lieutenant nodded.

"Hm. That's right, of course. I thought you understood that. The answer is obvious. Whoever it was killed Simon, did his best to make sure that the rose shower would be used. In a way he *forced* it on Simon, instead of allowing the man a free choice of all those bathing machines he had at his disposal. It was a good deal like forcing a card on someone, when you're doing parlor tricks."

Connor shook his head, wordless. He did not see, at all.

"Fixed the lock just as Gildersleeve found out," continued Masters crisply. "Then, getting out of the way, the killer left the door to the rose shower standing *wide open in invitation!* Don't you see? Any man whose mind was not positively obsessed with having a swim, or getting electrically tickled, would be apt to walk right into the rose shower, turn on the water, and slam the door.

"That was why the lock only clicked back and forth *once*—why the screw was of some use to the killer! Also it goes a little further, and shows that the murderer wanted to finish up his job soon, even if he could not make his deed simultaneous with the ending of the running grains of sand in the hour-glass.

"So now let's go a little further with what we are sure of.

"First, Simon Corlaes was wealthy. Just what condition his fortune may be in at the present time, I can't say; but he and his brother were rich as long ago as 1908, inheriting from their father, old Roger Corlaes. Simon, at least, has made millions since. He was a bear on Wall Street all through 1930, for one thing. And then his gas processes—ever since his father and he conducted that liquid-oxygen blasting for the Simplon Tunnel in 1899–1900—have made several more comfortable fortunes. I'll mention just those things he's done with xenon, krypton, neon, argon and nitrogen—all gases taken from the air, and then liquefied, you'll notice—as examples. And processes stolen from the actual inventors...

"Second, he had a brother who is said to have committed suicide. I don't believe that. Alfred Corlaes was murdered. And I think that murder was just the first step in a deeply thought-out plan for securing the Corlaes fortune!"

"Oh, but how could killing a valet, a chauffeur, and the maid of a dancing girl, fit into that?" protested the policeman, setting down his stein with the pewter cap raised. From the pantry door Sorenson came forward at once, whisked away the stein, and brought it back in a moment with a foaming collar.

"Leaving up the cap is a signal," grinned Masters. "I should think you could stand a few steins, though. But on this matter of all the other violence, let me go ahead.

"Third, Simon Corlaes left a will which probably was a freak of some kind. He didn't show it even to his lawyer; and the witnesses signed it without reading it. Simon hinted that the provisions of the will would be most unwelcome to people who might think they had something coming at his death. He kept the will in that safe in his apartment. It's gone now. The safe is empty.

"Oh, yes—" Masters raised a hand. "You might have the fingerprint squad go over that, though I'm sure it's no use. Our chief murderer, at any rate, had to use gloves for some of his work, and probably wore 'em all the time.

"The murderer of Simon had some reason to get away with the will. That means, probably, that with Simon dead intestate, the killer will inherit at least a part of the fortune."

"But *that* means young Marshall Corlaes, the adopted son!" interjected Connor with sudden interest. "Let's see, Masters. He was in Dutch with the old man. Why wouldn't he have a perfect motive for killing, and also for stealing the will—one which probably cut him off with a dollar and a damn?"

"I'm not denying that," said the detective soberly. "As it stands right now we have a circumstantial case against young Corlaes, but put him aside for a minute.

"When this lawn fete and general hooraw to celebrate the supposed end of the depression started last night, the plan for eliminating Simon Corlaes was all made.

But there was something else—something due to happen, which made the killer *warn* Simon!

"Even if the old man's death did not come off on hour glass schedule—and I don't think there was any real hope that it would do so—the mere fact that Simon was scared out of his wits meant a whole lot to someone!"

"I get you," nodded Connor slowly. "The killer stole the will at the same time he planted the warning. A change in the will right then, maybe, would sock him so much harder he just simply had to take a chance on the chair? That what you mean?"

"Perhaps. When the lawyer—Binney, is that his name?—gets here, we may hear something on that. Mrs. Mallen says that Simon had a peculiar taste in lawyers, and that Binney isn't precisely an ornament to the bar."

Then Masters, saying briefly that he was going to question Marshall Corlaes and the dancing girl, turned toward the stairs and made his way to the room where he had left this interesting couple together.

12

UNDER THE FUME HOOD

SUCCESS IN THE matter of solving the trap-lock to the rose shower, had made a different man out of Tom Gildersleeve. Heretofore he never had contributed an idea to one of Jigger Masters' cases, simply doing routine, and getting his satisfaction vicariously from his chief's success. Now he actually had used his own brain constructively, and with it a bit of the mechanical ingenuity which had made him a fair service station mechanic prior to helping his present employer on a case where an automobile figured prominently.

Now, left alone in the living room of Simon's apartment, the ruddy-faced ex-mechanic was far from content to lift his heels to the table and call it a day. With his chocolate-colored meerschaum exuding a fragrant trail of blended Samsoun Sert, Moudi and Latakia—the expensive super-mixture Simon had used in his hubbly-bubblies—Gildersleeve paced slowly up and down over the enormous Kermanshah rug.

His obtuse jaw projected a little. There was a frown denoting intense concentration on his forehead.

He had made no discoveries at all, prior to the time some weary fingerprint men, disgusted with the sameness and lack of result on this case, came up as a result of a hurried behest of the lieutenant. They asked Gildersleeve to show them the wall safe, but he knew nothing of it.

"Well, it's somewheres behind them top rows of books," said one of the men surlily. "I s'pose we can get it in time."

In time they did, and their results were just as juiceless as before. A few stale and blurred prints that were undoubtedly Simon's showed on the door. No prints at all on the dial. A blurred smudge which might have been the thumb of Jigger Masters—or the left ear of the Sultan of Sulu—came up on the glass of the next-to-top bookshelf. A grand total of zero.

"All I hope is that this bozo keeps on robbin' an' killin' till he wears out them gloves!" one of the disgruntled men growled, packing up his apparatus.

"An' 'en sprains his ankle an' has to walk on his hands!" supplemented another. "I ain't been home since night before last. Mebbe I got a wife still. I dunno…"

Gildersleeve grinned at them, but when they had decamped he became thoughtful. The not-very-secret safe with its bookshelf screen had given him an idea. Why not some more sliding panels, secret doors, and mysterious passages? He had been an avid reader of mystery stories, and from them had garnered the notion that almost all criminals with brains went to England when they felt the urge of a murder masterpiece.

Over there they usually selected an ancient castle said to be haunted…

Well, what was to have prevented old Simon Corlaes from having folding staircases, secret elevators, spyholes to be reached by crawling along secret passages? From all that was known of the man, he was furtive and lecherous both.

Gildersleeve started right in with Simon's bedroom, and hunted. He found nothing. But when he got to the living room he did make a pair of discoveries which were to assume real importance.

THE FIRST WAS a small pearl button, inconspicuously set in the molding at the west side of the fireplace. The floor space just here was occupied only by a floor lamp, and a straight chair which looked rather uncomfortable. None of the investigators had sat in it.

"Huh, what's this, a buzzer for the valet?" questioned Gildersleeve to himself. He pressed the button.

Whopp!

A wall panel, shoved by a stiff steel spring, leapt outward to the horizontal, striking his leg and startling him enough so he backed away quickly and grabbed at the butt of the revolver in his hip pocket.

There proved to be nothing devilish concealed there, however. The horizontal door could be shoved back into the wall, out of the way. From the aperture thus made, a typewriter stand pulled out and clicked into correct position.

On this stand were two articles, a French phone and a typewriter covered with a black dust-hood. Gildersleeve correctly surmised that the phone was Simon's unlisted private wire to the outside world.

Lifting the typewriter hood, the detective saw the machine to be an ordinary standard make in good condition, an Underwood No. 5. Not the latest model, but one probably used very occasionally, and which might have been standing in this place a long time without needing as much as a new ribbon.

Probably old Simon typed some of his own notes here, reflected Gildersleeve, remembering that there had been no secretary—unless Henry Handley Oliver sometimes acted in that capacity.

Without straining his new-found sleuthing ability in the slightest, Gildersleeve jumped to the hypothesis that this was where the warning note to Simon Corlaes had been written. Indeed, the shift lock was still depressed. The letter had been written all in capitals.

To prove or disprove his guess, Gildersleeve cast about for paper. He found a box containing ordinary 8½ x 11 bond, in the center drawer of the long table which stood in the middle of the room.

Inserting a sheet, the detective painstakingly picked out letters with one finger, typing the message from memory:

WHEN THE SAND GRAINS STOP RUNNING,
YOU WILL DIE!

"I'll bet three cents cash it's the same, when we put the letters under the glass!" he exclaimed proudly. There was a whole lot in this detective business, after all, if a fella had brains. Yanking out the sheet he placed it on the long table. Something more to show the boss. Well, it was a good day. Now, how about some more mysterious stuff?

He scowled up at the bookcases. On the other side of the wall against which they were built, he knew there was Simon's private laboratory. That room was bounded on the south by Simon's bathroom. The other rooms opened one into the other. Why shouldn't there be some kind of a door between the living room and laboratory? Didn't seem to make sense that a fella'd have his typewriter here where he made his experimental notes, and then have to shag around out into the hall to get to where his experiment itself was going on…

Simple trial and error this time brought speedy results. Having watched while the fingerprint men opened the dummy shelves above to get at the wall safe, Gildersleeve started on the knobs of other shelves, twisting them in the same fashion.

One of the knobs at the height of his chest turned all the way around. Exerting a pull, the thrilled detective brought a six-foot vertical section of five shelves out into the room toward him! And through the doorway thus opened, he stared straight across the zinc-topped tables of the laboratory, to the four windows facing west.

RESISTING A TEMPTATION to go immediately to Masters with these discoveries, Gildersleeve walked on tiptoe into the laboratory. He crouched a little, holding his breath and listening—hearing nothing at all. The laboratory was practically soundproof, and sealed against offensive odors, as far as the rest of the house was concerned.

Putting on his gloves, he went over to the low, wide metal cabinet housing the gas-liquefier. Possibly there were sinister articles stored in these places. Masters had found the flask of liquid air in one.

Careful of the extreme cold which swept out instantly when the handscrews were released and each door opened in turn, Gildersleeve took a quick look into the three compartments. He saw heavy, slow-moving parts, none of them now in motion, and vats with covered pipes leading in and out.

All of this was built-in, however, and no doubt was just what it claimed to be, a cascade system for producing extreme low temperatures. As long as the doors were kept tightly closed, the temperature within rose steadily but slowly, even when refrigeration itself had ceased.

Nothing of a chemist or toxicologist, Masters' chunky assistant looked over the wide, orderly rows of reagents on top of the metal cabinet, with suspicion.

"Looks like enough dope to poison an army," he growled.

In this he was perfectly correct. There were three long rows of nearly untouched bottles, which included many rare, and nearly all of the common poisons known to the pharmacopoeia.

Having a disinclination to touch what he did not understand, Gildersleeve soon left the chemicals to themselves. The rest of the laboratory looked to be of slight interest. He scanned the tables closely, seeing small apparatus for which the common use was easy enough to guess, but nothing at all striking.

The sinks and wash vats, with two exceptions, were open and empty, the drain plugs removed. Over two of the big vats, however, fume hoods which lowered on chains, and which had vents of flexible pipe giving into a wall flue, were down in position.

Gildersleeve felt at home with the sprocket and crank— not unlike the pedal and sprocket wheel of a bicycle— which gave leverage sufficient so the heavy fume hood could be raised and lowered by hand. He turned the wheel, raised the first hood, and saw that the space below was empty. Running it up and down two or three times more, he admired the way in which the heavy metal hood fitted over the three-foot basin beneath.

Then, without much interest, he moved over to the second fume-hooded vat, which was a duplicate of the first. Here the hood resisted his efforts. Something held it, not tight to the vat, but about eight inches above it. Holding the lever so it would not spin back, Gildersleeve bent down so he could peer into the narrow horizontal opening.

Then a choked cry burst from his lips. Blue eyes wide, he straightened half way, and put both hands, and the full strength of his bunchy shoulders into turning the wheel.

The hood rose slowly, reluctantly; and as it came up to the level of his eyes, something heavy and limp inside the vat changed position and came along with the fume hood, making a dull, sodden sound!

When the hood would rise no further, the detective reached around and got his revolver. He thrust the barrel of this weapon between the chain and the toothed sprocket, so it could not fly back. Then he thrust in both arms, attempting to draw out the heavy, sticky-wet thing which dangled there. And not succeeding!

"Great jumpin' Sigisimond Planus!" he swore shakily, drawing out his broad hands and staring at the blood upon them. His face had paled from its ruddy hue.

"An' it's *another* dead one, b'God—*a corpse that's still warm!*" he breathed explosively.

13

THE PERVERSE ALIBI

THREE-QUARTERS OF AN hour prior to Gildersleeve's shocking discovery under the fume hood, Jigger Masters knocked on the door of the chamber where young Marshall Corlaes and the dancer, Dorothy Graham, had gone for their few minutes of confidential talk. That the few minutes had lengthened into thirty came as an abrupt surprise to both.

At Masters' knock on the door, the girl and young man looked up blankly. Dorothy Graham was frightened.

"Oh, are you going to tell him?" she whispered.

"Tell him nothing!" said Corlaes. "You are out of the picture, and I'm going to keep you out."

He shook his head decisively, and opened the door.

Masters came in with a curt nod, motioning Dorothy to keep her place in the window where she had been seated. He carried a chair from the room for himself.

"Now I hope everything's settled between you two," he began, as Corlaes sat down on the end of the window seat, taking out a cigarette case. He proffered smokes to the girl and Masters, both refusing, whereupon he lighted one for himself.

"Why, it is," answered Corlaes quietly. "The matter that

was bothering Miss Graham is one that has no bearing on your problem—except it might reflect on the character of a dead man. And, incidentally, it might cause Dor—Miss Graham's reputation to suffer. I'm advising her just to sit tight!"

Masters folded his arms, regarding the youth sardonically. "I wish I could just sit tight, too!" he snapped. "Look here. A reputation is a swell thing. Mine is gone, even with myself—but no matter. What concerns you two is just this. You are both in danger of being murdered. Either that—*or one of you is the murderer!*" He glared now at Marshall Corlaes.

"Oh, bosh, I don't believe it," said the young man. Yet he shifted uneasily, casting a worried look at the girl.

"You'll either talk now, both of you, or I'll have Connor arrest you for murder—right today!" He rose, and frowned straight down on Marshall Corlaes.

"I warn you that there is what amounts to a water-tight case against you. And maybe I could strengthen it still further, by delving back into your past!"

"Oh, shucks," surrendered Corlaes with a wry grin. "You'd just be making a fool of yourself. But if Dorothy says to tell you now—"

"Of course I do!" she broke in impulsively. "It would be terrible to have you arrested. These—these happenings, Mr. Masters," she continued, taking over the tale herself, "are no more than have happened to me many times in the course of my work as a *danseuse*. One grows to expect them.

"The one you want to know about, I think, really amounted to nothing at all. Simon Corlaes tried to get into the chamber I used for dressing, about ten o'clock last night, when I was just about to get ready. My mother held him at the door. Then Marshall"—she colored slightly, but did not correct herself—"came along, and persuaded old Simon to leave me alone."

"Another fist fight?" queried Masters, addressing Corlaes.

"Oh-ho, you heard about that time? No, this was no fight. Simon knew me too well by now. He ran like a whipped cur. I'd have punched him gladly, only I got no chance."

"What were you doing in this house at all? I understood that you were not allowed here, after that time you pummeled Simon."

Marshall Corlaes grinned sourly. "Oh, I was allowed, all right," he said. "That old lecher would even have taken me back like a prodigal son, except I wouldn't have it. I came to the manor any time I wanted to. Just managed to come when Simon wasn't here; that's all. Last night I had a strong reason."

His eyes swung to Dorothy.

"I had seen Dorothy a number of times, though I just never tried to get to know her. Last night I came determined. I'd found I—I *had* to make her acquaintance!"

"There—there was one other thing, possibly more important," the girl broke in, her color heightened. "You'll have to judge. I pawned a blush pearl necklace for Mrs. Mallen!"

This was a new one on Masters, and he listened intently. The girl said that the matter had come up suddenly. Mrs. Mallen had found it imperative to get eight thousand dollars in cash immediately. She could not wait to go to her strong box or her bank in town.

"IT WAS IMPROMPTU, I'm sure," said Dorothy. "She had got a phoned acceptance to her party, and a dun on a bridge debt at the same time. She was fairly crimson with anger when she came to my room. Mother and I were just unpacking. Mrs. Mallen took me aside and whispered. She knew where to get the money—from a fellow named Sanine. Would I go with her and transact the business? She would wait in the car for me. She did not want even her own maid to know. That was why she asked me, a stranger, to do it. She promised me an extra hundred dollars. So I did it."

"You got the eight thousand dollars—from Sanine?" queried Masters, a slight edge of incredulity in his voice. He knew the roadhouse pawnbroker, whose real name was Kalenderian. He was a tough customer.

"Yes—after a long argument," said Dorothy. "I gave it and the ticket to Mrs. Mallen. We came back here. That's all."

"Not quite all, perhaps," added Marshall quietly. "I see you're a trifle skeptical about the sum, Mr. Masters. Well, that was the famous blush pearl necklace. It's insured for $150,000!

"But I see something funny, just the same. Probably irrelevant, but it interests me just the same. Stella said she owed eight thousand on a bridge debt. Holy mackerel, that is certainly a lie! Stella can play a dumb enough game of auction, but she's never even learned contract bridge. And she never gambles at all.

"Also, she constitutionally hates to owe anybody

anything. So, what was her reason for needing eight grand all of a sudden? Simon would pay the party expenses by check, of course. I can't imagine any reason she'd have— unless she's taken to supporting Lacey Glendon. She's been playing around some with him lately; and Lacey is always in money trouble, of course. There's a rumor that he's in trouble over checks, though I don't know any details.

"But I think Stella would have too much sense to get in deep with Lacey. He's a rotter, and I've heard her tell him that to his face.

"Now, I'd like to ask you, Mr. Masters, if you won't keep mum about Simon and his raid on Dorothy's dressing room. You can do that for a while, anyway, can't you? I'm a lot more worth while as a suspect than she is. I was rooting around this place all last evening. I don't think I could muster up an alibi for any given ten minutes!"

Masters nodded thoughtfully. If Stella Mallen corroborated the matter of jewel pawning, then there was little to connect Dorothy Graham with any of these people.

According to the story thus far, Marshall would have to go under the closest scrutiny, however.

The detective gave no hint of his disturbing thoughts. He secretly had come to like this clear-eyed young man. Also the simplicity and directness of his sudden attachment for the dancer had its appeal.

But the detective's work had to be impersonal. He knew with inward alarm that right this minute, if he were to draw up the obvious circumstantial indictment against Marshall Corlaes, and present it to the District Attorney of Nassau County, the police would look no further.

Indeed, it would appear shockingly plain that there was

no need to look further. Right on the scene all the while. By his own admission possessing sufficient motive. Particularly, no one knew thus far, at any rate, just where he had been at the minute Simon had stepped into the lethal shower bath. Presumably Marshall had gone to bed in this very room. But it would be easy enough to sneak across the hall, enter the laboratory, do the job, and then mingle inconspicuously with the crowd of guests in the corridor. Masters had a lurking suspicion that the policeman who had been up with Glendon, had not been awake to any other happening on the floor. And there was no reason at that time for the guard to suspect another killing to be due, as far as that went.

Further, Marshall Corlaes had known all along about the set of antique hour glasses. He had been a member of this household until just about the time Alfred Corlaes was found with an hour glass and a fired revolver in front of him. Marshall himself had shown that he was used to getting in and out of the house without disturbing guests or members of the family. He could have got in that way, and killed Alfred.

Oh, on paper it would be convincing enough. Even more so if thundered forth in a courtroom by a good prosecutor. Probably the death of Haines, the chauffeur, and the assault upon Lacey Glendon would fall in line; though, the other circumstances were so damning that in all probability these happenings in the garage would not necessarily have to be explained, in order to win a conviction on the main charges.

"I'm surely glad you've been frank with me, and I want to thank both of you," said Masters.

"By the way, there is just one more thing now," he added. "It may be painful—"

"Well?" Marshall's face had clouded. "If it's what I guess you'll ask—"

"Without a doubt it is," nodded Masters soberly. "I want to know, Mr. Corlaes, just what it was that brought about the fist fight between you and Simon Corlaes—the one in which Edward Green had to interfere?"

A veritable Jekyll-Hyde change flashed into the hitherto pleasant features of the young man! As though stabbed by an unbearable pain of hurt and rage, he sprang to his feet, fists clenching.

"Damn you, I won't answer! And if you—" he gritted out, advancing a step toward the detective, who remained motionless in the chair.

Instantly the dancer was between them, hands on his upper arms, forcing Marshall back. Masters quietly rose to his feet, intending to waive the question for the time being. He had guessed it probably was one which young Corlaes would hate to have dragged out in front of strangers. Yet— it would be the first thing a coroner would want to know. And Marshall Corlaes might as well get used to the grim idea that he was under suspicion; then the actuality would not come as so terrible a shock.

"Don't, please!" cried the girl. "Don't, Marshall! This man—Mr. Masters is trying to help us, I know!"

For a long moment the fury burned in the youth's eyes. Then they gradually lowered to the upturned face of the girl, and his fists unclenched.

"I'm sorry," the youth said in a husky voice.

Then, as if it had been the most natural thing in the

world, he placed both hands under her elbows, leaned back slightly, lifted her clear of the floor, and kissed her on the lips!

Beyond a slight gasp of surprise, and possibly a momentary stiffening of her slender body, the girl made no sign. When he lowered her again to the floor, she stood looking up at him gravely, an odd expression of mingled fright and inevitability in her dark eyes.

"I WILL ANSWER that in front of Dorothy, Mr. Masters," said Marshall quietly enough then. "I would have told her anyhow, when the time came I could do myself the honor of asking her to be my wife.

"It's a horrible thing. One of the reasons why I'll never cheer when the police take the killer of Simon Corlaes. And there are many such reasons which many other men could advance. Simon Corlaes was a thief and a beast. I hope also he was a damned liar. This thing happened some twenty-four years ago. There was a young chemist, a graduate of M.I.T. His name was John Vandervoort. In 1897 he invented a process for fumeless blasting, a valuable thing in mines or railroad tunnels, you can see. Vandervoort perfected this process for making blasting cartridges out of lampblack or gasblack saturated with liquid oxygen. When the cartridges were fresh they were practically as powerful as an equal weight of dynamite. And they gave off no poisonous gases.

"I won't bother with any more of that. You can look it up if you care about it. Vandervoort had a partner, another young man named Stanley Kershaw—"

Here Jigger Masters stiffened. The scent suddenly had grown hot!

"To shorten a long, sordid story, Kershaw sold out his partner. He went in with Roger Corlaes and that old fellow's two sons, Alfred and Simon. Vandervoort was left holding an empty bag. And I think that a little later Kershaw got what he deserved, being bilked of his share by the precious Corlaes tribe! The process had not been patented then. In fact, there were no patents taken out on it until later, when they worked out a way to keep the cartridges fresh long enough so they could be transported and used with greater ease.

"The only thing Vandervoort got out of it, was employment for a short time."

"Like Henry Handley Oliver?" suggested Masters.

"Yes, like Oliver, poor devil," nodded Corlaes. "Well, Vandervoort was married to my mother. There came an 'accidental' explosion in the Corlaes laboratory, and then my mother was a widow—just a few months before I was born. She died, also, less than a year after I put in an appearance.

"And the thing which brought about my fight with Simon Corlaes, which made me leave this house and refuse formal adoption and any more allowance from him, was that old devil calmly telling me that my supposed father committed suicide—and that he, Simon Corlaes, was my real father, anyhow!"

"Oh, he lied!" breathed Dorothy Graham. "You *never* could have had him for a father. I *know!*"

"I hope you're right," he said gently, sadly. "But there's no way of knowing. If you *will* marry me, you'll be taking a nameless wretch—"

"Hush! I'll think about it," she said, placing a hand over

his mouth. "And besides, I think it's just grand—about us, I mean. Why, we'll be able to pick out any old name we happen to like—after we're married!" There was a half-sob, half-laugh in the last words.

Masters made a strangled noise, and turned toward the door, shaking his head. This was almost more than he could hope to chew and swallow all in one mouthful. Love, death, lust, mystery—*and alibi!*

"Hm!" he observed, turning back at the door. "So you actually mean to stand there and tell me, Marshall Whatever-You're-Going-To-Choose-For-A-Name," he asked sardonically, "that you never *have* been legally adopted? That, in fact, unless Simon Corlaes left you something in that funny will, you won't get anything from his estate now?"

"I won't—and if he willed me anything, I'd drop it in the sewer, and hope he saw it washed away with all the rest of the filth!" said the young man with emphasis.

Masters believed him, and was able to grin one-sidedly. "All right," he chuckled dryly. "I'm congratulating you— on two points. First and most important, you've got a girl who has a sense of humor. Second, you've just helped me a lot. For hours I have been trying to pry out *some* argument to advance for your innocence of all these murders. And finding none. Now you've let drop—quite casually of course—the one reason why the District Attorney *won't* dare to arrest you for a day or two, anyhow!"

But Masters was a little precipitate. Another reason was coming toward him at that very minute. And Tom Gildersleeve was bringing it.

14

NOBODY KILLED THIS MAN!

"**COME THIS WAY,** Chief! Quick!"

Tom Gildersleeve stopped in the corridor, midway between the open laboratory door, and the room beyond the main staircase from which Masters emerged. He beckoned excitedly.

"It's another murder—a man," he said in a hoarse whisper, when Jigger Masters came at a quick stride. "An' this one ain't been dead more'n a few minutes. Found him there in the lab, He's stuck in one of them vats. Couldn't get him out easy. Thought you'd better see, before I hauled him away—"

Masters halted at the laboratory door, looking in briefly to see the raised fume hood and a suggestion of the body imprisoned there. Then he issued crisp orders.

"Get Connor. Phone Cortelyou, if he's gone back. Then check immediately on every damn person in this place! The most of them—except Glendon—ought to be downstairs together. I'll see about Glendon first, myself."

Lacey Glendon was in bed, asleep. Barnes, who came to the door in answer to Masters' knock, testified simply that the man he had been left to watch had not opened his eyes for an hour; had not been up since Dr. Herschel left. It was quite impossible that he had committed any recent murder.

"Is it something more, Chief?" asked Barnes respectfully; but his eyes were wide. He and Gildersleeve never had been in the midst of an avalanche of gory crime such as this.

"Yes—something more," grated Masters. "Tell you, Barnes," he went on. "Lock Glendon in, and come along with me. I'll need help, probably."

Barnes took a key from his pocket and complied. But then Masters had another idea. "Go to Mrs. Mallen's apartment—there, that's the door over there—and see if anyone is inside. She ought to be downstairs, but possibly she isn't. Then join me in the lab." He turned into the open doorway, and drew the door almost closed behind him.

At first touch of the body so queerly suspended there from the fume hood, the detective felt the body warmth. A muffled exclamation burst from his lips. Why, the man might not be dead at all!

Reaching in and up, Masters discovered shortly how it was that the body hung from the hood in this fashion. The fume hood itself, while oblong at the bottom to fit the vat, tapered upward and became rounded, growing smaller as it led to the wall flue. Its shape was not unlike an old-fashioned phonograph horn, though the small-diametered upper part was brass flex, to allow free movement when the hood was raised and lowered.

The victim's head was curious in shape, being short from forehead to occiput, almost round, and very high and tapering upward from the plane of nose bridge to the crown. As if he gloried in accentuating this peculiarity, which was next thing to a deformity, the man had his hair cut in the old way known as pompadour, clippers up the back making his head seem chopped off abruptly there.

The head had jammed so tightly into the narrowing fume hood, that it took all the strength of Masters' fingers to jerk it away. Then, however, as Barnes hurried up—telling in a rapid sentence that Mrs. Mallen was in her room, having Elsie Fenlon, her maid, wave her hair—the detective managed to get a hold under the victim's arms, and drag him out of the vat to the laboratory floor.

It became instantly apparent why the man with the chimney-like head lay there limp and seemingly lifeless. He was dressed in lightweight black serge, but wore a high wing collar and black tie with white silk shirt. Just above the bloodstained collar, and below his small, lobe-less ear was what appeared at first glance to be a rosette or machined metal flower.

It was not exactly that, as Masters determined at once. It was the cheaply ornate base of a common needle file, the sort of upright spike on which people impale notes and scribbled data. The spike, which seemed to be about eight inches in length, had been driven with great force straight through the center of the wrinkled, rope-like neck, and had pierced the collar on the other side. There was blood all down the front of the man's shirt; and his trousers were saturated with it.

Still, it was evident that this was not blood enough to suggest a pierced carotid artery or jugular vein.

Masters garnered these details almost automatically, while he worked hard to discover the faintest sign of life. There was none. Though the body heat, faded scarcely at all from normal temperature, told that life had not been gone as long as one hour, the man was undoubtedly dead. Looking at the downward and sidewise slant of the ugly needle, Masters guessed that it had pierced the pharynx. Likely enough the poor fellow had slowly suffocated in his own blood!

THROUGH THE TIME of routine tasks, performed by photographers, finger-print men, the medical examiner and Connor with his aides, Masters held moodily aloof. He paced up and down the other side of the laboratory, arms behind his back, reviewing all the grim chronology of the crimes.

Gildersleeve watched him, the blue eyes worried. After a time he ventured to speak.

"Don't take it too hard, Chief," he said. "After all, we only been playin' around this dump part of a day. You spent nearly six weeks nailin' that sedan killer—but you got him."

Gildersleeve grinned cheerfully. "C'mon in through here—an' take a look at the doorway while you come," he invited proudly. "It'll mebbe soothe you some to know I was monkey-fugglin' around right next door, lookin' for secret passages an' such, all the time that old guy with the two-story dome was gettin' shivved. An' I didn't hear as much as a pip-squeak."

For a half-second Masters stared thoughtfully, but then followed his assistant through the bookcase doorway into the living room of Simon's suite. He nodded briefly a tentative recognition of the capital letters typed on the Underwood machine. But all the while it seemed that the detective's mind was detached, racing back through a maze of foregoing circumstances, endeavoring to fit the details of previous killings with an odd new possibility which had suggested itself to him.

Connor, looking half-dead with worry and lack of sleep, came in then. Masters briefly showed him the typewriter, crediting Gildersleeve with the discovery; but the police lieutenant seemed apathetic.

"This gives me another man back," he said miserably. "We don't have to hunt any more for Stanley Kershaw. That's him—found out from his driving license and some papers in his pocket."

Masters took a deep breath. So this was John Vander-voort's partner, the once-young betrayer who had conspired with the Corlaes men to steal the oxygen-blast-ing process—and then had been cheated in turn. It was impossible to feel any deep indignation over his death, or indeed any regret, except for what he might have told had he remained alive. The one burning need right now was to improvise some adequate catch-as-catch-can theory which would tie the murderer's hands before he could go further with his slaughter. Even actual, convincing proof which would send him to the electric chair for what he had done up to now, might have to wait.

"Hold up, Connor," bade Masters, as the lieutenant started back toward the noisy laboratory, shoulders sagging with weariness and bafflement. "I sent Gil down to check on the whereabouts of the servants and guests. Sent him down as soon as I heard about this happening. What about it, Gil?"

The ruddy-faced man shrugged. "There ain't been a servant come upstairs, except Elsie Fenlon. Mrs. Mallen got her to come up an' do her hair. All the guests have been in a huddle down in the east drawin' room, since that dancer's maid's murder. All except young Corlaes an' the dancin' girl—an' they been with you. Oh, yeah, an' Glendon. But Barnes is right there with him."

"That's right about Glendon and the other two. Also, I know Mrs. Mallen is getting a finger-wave, and I'm convinced she and her maid have been right where they said they'd been, in her apartment. Take a look at these names on the servants' timecards, Gil." Masters hauled out the sheaf of signed statements. "You're sure all these were down there?"

Gildersleeve nodded. "Yeah, they're all down in the kitchen. Sorenson's the only one that's moved up front as far as the guests. I'll bet you couldn't coax the rest away from each other. They're scairt."

"Lord, who wouldn't be!" said Connor. "I almost wish he'd choose me next—before the D.A. gets here. I got an orderly mind, and like to have things where they belong. The place to catch hell is in hell, not here."

"Then, here's a list of the people down in the drawin' room, Chief," said Gildersleeve. "You ain't questioned some of 'em yet; but I asked each one if he or she'd been away. Then I asked the others about each one. It all jibed. They all been right there together—like sheep in a pen in the stockyards."

The brief list read as follows:

1.   H.H. Oliver (H_2O). Been playing radio real soft. Hasn't gone out at all.
2.   Eloise Gunter. Talking to Oliver. Been out once about three minutes, with mother.

3. Mrs. P. Gunter. Laying down on sofa. All in. Looks real sick. Been out once, daughter says. No use suspecting this old lady.

4. Mr. & Mrs. L. Carmichael. This is the Carmichael family who helped sink that big investment banking house. I'd like to help fry the Mr., my old man losing six thousand bucks. But the Carmichaels are contract players and good sitters. They ain't been out.

5. Louis LeFevre. Canuck, who lost one arm in war. Nervous fella. Been out five-six times. Maybe is a dope, but I don't see how he could do much killing with his left hand.

6. Henry Otto Black. Named Schwartz till '17. Rich baker with a big pod taking up his lap. Has been eating pretzels and drinking beer. Out once. Couldn't get him excited in an earthquake. Friend of Simon's. Maybe.

7. Two Black daughters & Missus. Up and coming ladies. Good lookers. All been out once, together. Want to play cards now, but can't get fourth. Don't look guilty to me.

8. Leland Stanford Lessington. Here's your suspect. Says he's missing polo practice, but I'll bet he's a secret crooner. Been out once. Acts kind of sweet on the youngest Black gal, but she kids him. Doesn't play cards or smoke or swear. Probably horrid to his old mother. Naw!

"I HAVEN'T QUESTIONED any of them yet," said Masters with a grimace, folding the sheet. "But I doubt that it's necessary in most cases. This is the way I'm calling the turn at the moment, Connor.

"We have one crime which suggests a woman, or an effeminate sort of man. I mean that poisoned rouge pot.

The other murders, however, demand a man's strength—
or that of an exceptionally strong and determined woman.
Lugging sixty pounds of Onnes flask with liquid air in
it, for instance. Lifting this body of Kershaw up into the
vat. Wielding a blackjack with strength enough to smash
a man's skull. Even jabbing that needle file clear through
Kershaw's neck and the linen collar beyond. One of those
things just *might* have been done by a furious, well-setup
woman. But it's nonsense to think of a woman doing them
all. They are simply too unfeminine. No, I'm looking for a
man—and not a one-armed man like LeFevre, a pot-bel-
lied baker and beer-drinker like Black, or a sixty-year-old
crooked financier like Carmichael, either.

"By the way, Gil. Go right now over to Marshall Corlaes'
room. Tell him and that young sweetheart of his I want
them both to go down and stay with the others. I don't
believe anyone would try to kill them while they're both
together, but the murderer might not know they were
together, and have to make a try for both instead of one."

"Good Lord!" exclaimed Connor. "You think there will
be more? Why, damn it all, there *can't* be! Every single
person on these grounds—even the gatekeeper and the
farmers, 'way out at the ends of the place—are watched.
They—"

"Go back to Glendon, Barnes," Masters said, seeing the
smaller of his assistants looking in through the bookcase
door. "Stay with him, unless he feels well enough to go
down with the others. In that case, make sure he under-
stands he must stay with them every minute.

"Gil, you go tell Mrs. Mallen that as soon as her hair-do

is finished, I want her down there, too. The maid must go back with the servants."

"All right, Chief," grinned Gildersleeve. "If you find a bleedin' detective layin' in the hallway, you'll know I told her your message. That fair lady likes me not, ever since I embraced her in Glendon's room, an' dumped her back out into the corridor."

He filled his meerschaum with the mixture from Simon's humidor, lighted the pipe, and went cheerfully on his errand across the hall.

"That doggoned Mallen woman," suddenly said Connor. "Sure she isn't strong enough to fit, Jigger? I phoned Sanine, you know. He says that Mrs. Mallen sent the necklace down to him, and he lent eight thousand dollars on it!"

"The worst I can suspect Mrs. Mallen of, is that rouge pot poisoning—and then possible complicity in the other killings. I want a man for Simon's murder, though. Stella Mallen won't do. In the first place she doesn't know enough to handle liquid air, or I'm greatly mistaken."

"Well, heavens above," said Connor with a trace of petulance, "even a woman can only get fried once. If you nail her as an accessory, and then pin that cyanide poisoning on her—"

"I'll come back to that with you," interrupted Masters. "I see Cortelyou's going. Just one thing to chew on for the moment, though. Young Marshall Corlaes never was adopted by Simon, and has no reason to expect anything under Simon's will—if that instrument ever is found. That probably makes Mrs. Stella Mallen the next of kin!"

"Oh-ho!" said Connor with a falling intonation. "The

li'l girl inherits if the will isn't found, does she? Huh, I've a good mind to—"

But Masters had gone into the laboratory, where he had chanced to see Cortelyou doffing his white jacket, preparatory to dressing in street clothes and leaving.

The medical examiner gave the tall detective a stony glare. "What a piece of cheese you turned out to be!" he snarled. "Are there any more victims scheduled? If there are, I'd like to rent a room right here. I'm using up more gas, running back and forth now from Mineola, than my county salary will buy. And autopsies and inquests! Damn! I've got the next week booked solid now, and—"

Masters was pacific, because he had a somewhat irregular favor to ask. He soothed him in the old-fashioned, certain way, by pointing out how much worse off Connor and he were. The medical examiner, at any rate, need fear nothing worse than a few full days. He was not likely to fail...

"How long do you think this man Kershaw has been dead, Doctor?" Masters inquired.

Cortelyou growled. "Who could tell exactly?" he demanded. "It's fairly warm weather. Cooling would be slow. As a matter of fact, there had been a cooling of less than one degree. No sign at all of rigor. Certainly not more than one hour from the time I started to examine. D'you mean you'd like the exact minute, maybe?" he ended with a trace of a sneer.

"No, Doctor," said Masters quietly. "I wonder, then, if you'd put this autopsy ahead—or part of it, anyhow?" he amended, as he saw Cortelyou's face darken with negation.

"It's of the greatest importance for me to know just how Kershaw died—"

"Didn't that file spike look like enough cause? Would you like me to discover carbolic acid, arsenic and hyoscin in his stomach?"

"I don't mean that," said Masters patiently. "If you could dissect down into his neck, and see just what injury really was caused by the spike, we might hazard a guess at how long Kershaw could have lived *after being struck!*"

"That would make a difference to somebody, I suppose?"

"Life or death," said Masters briefly.

"Hm." The medico pursed his lips. He was neither fool nor charlatan, and saw that this detective was serious in the request. The doctor shed his suit coat again, and slipped into the jacket. "I left the spike file right in the wound," he said. "I rather wanted to see how it got through there without puncturing a big blood vessel, myself. I'll cut in right now, and we can see. It won't take more than fifteen minutes—though I'll have to be more thorough later, of course."

"THANK YOU," SAID Masters. "You see," he added, as the doctor took knives, scissors and probe from his bag, bending over the body of Kershaw, which had been put on a stretcher, atop one of the zinc tables, "up till this time, the actual moment of death in each case has been practically certain. Here for the first time it looks *un*certain—and trebly important!"

"Oh, I haven't a doubt it was practically instantaneous," replied Cortelyou, getting down to business. "But there are cases—hm!" He paused, bent closer, then did a little fine dissection of tissues with knife and probe. Masters did not question, but drew out a cigarette, lighted it, and strolled to the window.

Cortelyou could be trusted to do a good job, none better. And for the first time that day Masters himself realized that his whole frame ached with fatigue and strain.

"You've asked a hard question!" the doctor said after a time, straightening up. "Just what does it mean if I say this man died instantly?"

"Well, then," retorted Masters grimly, "nobody killed this man! You see, every single person in this house can account for an hour or more of his or her time, prior to the moment Gildersleeve found the body. So unless Gildersleeve himself did it—and he never saw or heard of the man before—it was suicide!"

"Well, it wasn't suicide," said Cortelyou. "Come here close and look. It is a most extraordinary stab. I'd never have believed it if I hadn't cut down myself.

"In the first place, it misses all important blood vessels. It pierces the glottis and one tonsil, before coming out. But before it gets to the glottis—look here!" He lifted a whitish, cordlike bit of tissue.

"This is the tenth cranial nerve. It runs the lungs, stomach, liver, spleen, diaphragm, and so on. And that spike went right straight through it, like a pin through a piece of twine! See? The nerve is almost as big as a lead pencil—see how it's pierced? Well, *that* ought to kill a man deader'n King Tut, being as you'd normally suppose it'd stop his heart, stop his breathing, stop the expansion and contraction of his spleen, and I don't know what-all. But all the same, it *didn't* kill him!

"How can I tell that? Look close. You can see there has

been bleeding for an inch, *inside the nerve sheath!* Dead nerves don't bleed. No, sir, your man may have lived ten minutes or ten hours, for all I know. The chances are, when I get down to the t. and a. dissection, I'll find that blood from the glottis trickled down the larynx, and slowly drowned the poor devil. It's likely that the nerve injury brought on some sympathetic akinesia—motor paralysis—so even if he became conscious there in the vat, he couldn't help himself."

"Sweet thought!" said Masters with a shiver. "Whatever wrongs he committed, that would be payment enough. But what you've told me fits in, Doctor. Many thanks, indeed!"

Then, without giving the medico chance to question him in turn, he hurried out to find Connor, who had stayed in the adjoining room, and now was getting a complaint concerning the treatment of three star crime reporters, phoned in by the district attorney.

"Let them languish a while!" snapped Masters. "Send out reports to the gate as often as you want to, but don't let that howling mob inside, under any circumstances."

The patrolman looked at Connor, who nodded wearily.

Then with a wry grin, the messenger went downstairs, to lift a shelved receiver and give a modified message to an angry man on the other end of the wire.

The angry man fairly exploded.

When the patrolman replaced the receiver, he was a trifle pale. Then he shrugged. The D.A. was an ambitious man. This action of jailing reporters who trespassed was bringing down on his head the wrath of all newspapers from the New York *Times* to the Hempstead *Sentinel*. So the D.A. was coming right over to end such nonsense.

Then the guillotine blade would fall. Connor was slated for retirement anyhow, so probably did not care. But the patrolman looked forward with a grim grin to the passage at arms which surely would occur between the D.A. and Jigger Masters. Where did a private dick get any authority, anyway?

But Masters was not wasting any worry on this score. Cautioning Connor on one point he had overlooked momentarily, he made sure that the lieutenant had not said and would not say anything to the papers or to his subordinates just now, concerning the matter of Marshall Corlaes' adoption.

Then Masters asked for a pot of black coffee—made by a policeman—and a tin of sardines or salmon, unopened.

"I'd love to slip away home for a bath, shave, clean clothes and a meal, Connor," he sighed, fingering his bristly chin, "but there's going to be no sleep or creature comfort for us. It's now four-thirty. Tell Barnes and Henry Handley Oliver to come up here. Between now and midnight we're going to have to fight this through and get our murderers."

"Or else what?" asked the police officer.

"Or else," said Masters grimly, "the flesh will triumph and we'll go to sleep on the job. In that event, unless I'm vastly mistaken, a number of those in this house will never see tomorrow's sun!"

15

A SMELL OF SMOKE

FOR REASONS HAVING to do more with the dancer,
Dorothy Graham, and Marshall Corlaes, than with the
actual murders which had occurred in the manor house
and garage, Stella Mallen took her maid with her to her
apartment, and stayed there a long time.

"I look as tough as if I'd just got saved at a camp meeting, Elsie," she said, emerging from the bathroom. "You
can start right in with my toes and work up. Along toward
the end I'll have a mud facial; then you can set and wave
this-here-now crowning beauty."

She shook her head and grimaced. Locks of wet
ash-blond hair swung around and stuck lifelessly to her
forehead. Before she stretched out on the cushioned chaise
longue for the chiropody, she poured out the last ounce of
rye whiskey from a pint bottle on the dressing table, and
swallowed it.

"Brr!" she shivered, and reached for cigarettes and
matches. "Somebody's bootleg is walking on my grave!"

"Moddom would like a glass of water?" inquired the
maid solicitously.

"Nope. There'll be lots of whiskey breaths in this house
before today's over. Go right ahead. I've got nothing but

time to waste, but oodles of that." She blew a long column of smoke toward the ceiling, and gathered the blue silk negligée a fold closer about her pink form.

Ninety minutes of chiropody, massage of the body, and a mud facial ensued, before Stella sat down in front of the dressing table for the hair wave. She grimaced vigorously into the mirror, getting rid of the masklike feeling in the skin of her face. Then she lit another cigarette, and smoked moodily while the expert maid worked. Gildersleeve came then with Masters' message, but Stella jeered and paid little attention to it.

"Tell me, Elsie," she said with such sudden energy that the maid started, lifting her hands away, "who d'you think's responsible for all this hell that's been raised? In other words, who d'you think bumped off Simon, and Ed Green, and Haines? Oh, yes, and that dancer's maid?"

"It isn't for the likes of me to say, Moddom," returned Elsie Fenlon, suddenly prim and cautious.

Stella looked at her in the glass. The pale blue eyes widened, then suddenly half-closed again in a sour grin. "Oh, all right, Elsie," Stella chuckled meaningly. "But if you weren't going to pick me, who would be your *next* choice? I really can't blame you for suspecting things, after the way I ranted around here about Simon, and Marshall, and the rest. But I really didn't do it, you know."

"Oh, no, Moddom! I was not thinking *that!* I just had an idea—" Here the maid halted in mid-sentence, and went on industriously at her task. Apparently she would never add to her words unless prodded.

"All right, name the scoundrel. I want to put a wreath on his brow—or his tombstone. I dunno just which," said the woman dryly. "There's murders and murders, you know, Elsie. Who's your hoss in this race? Go on, you can't make me sore. I'm only a selling plater."

"Well—" the maid looked about her, as if she expected crouching listeners to be scattered about the locked boudoir. "I don't know," she whispered breathlessly. "Only I—I wouldn't be surprised if it was Mr. Oliver who killed the master!"

"Huh?" Stella straightened in her chair, staring incredulously into the glass. "That redheaded sapsucker? Oh, hell, Elsie. Well, go on, girl. Tell me. When and how did H_2O rise above diluted blackmail? What makes you think he could ever do such a thing?"

The maid began to tremble. Only by dint of much insistence did Stella get the story. And then it made her want to grin and whistle all at once. Henry Handley Oliver certainly was in for a bad time, if Masters and Connor got hold of this tidbit!

Briefly stated, Elsie told of something her mistress had known for a long time. This was the surreptitious meeting of Henry Oliver and the girl to whom Simon had been engaged, the "little dish-faced simp" (Stella's contemptuous words), Eloise Gunter. Everyone connected with the ménage, Stella thought to herself many a time, knew of this love affair. Everyone but Simon—and at times Stella had suspected the man of deliberately shutting his eyes, so in time he could ease himself out. It would have been just Simon's cunning way, to let a man he hated think this thievery of a sweetheart would be a terrific blow—and then snicker up his sleeve, when he was released without a breach-of-promise suit.

"It was last week when you were out at Montauk, and sent me back here to get that blue bathing suit, Moddom," concluded Elsie breathlessly, her words tumbling out fast now. "There wasn't anyone here but Mr. Corlaes, Mrs. Gunter and Miss Eloise. But Miss Eloise said she had a headache, and came up to lie down a while after lunch. Mr. C-Corlaes came up to Mr. Oliver's room—he was s'posed to be in the city that day—and found Miss Eloise with Mr. Oliver! Oh, and did they quarrel!

"They hadn't seen me at all, since I came up here the back way. I heard p-part of it. It ended up with Mr. Oliver shouting at Mr. Corlaes, and telling him to shut up and say nothing, or he'd do for him proper. 'I've more than half a mind to bust you wide open anyhow!' Mr. Oliver said. 'You can't fire me and you know you can't! And you can't say a word about Eloise. You've got no witnesses, and she could take you for a million dollars!'"

That was when the maid had fled. She had told the story belowstairs, however, so there was small likelihood now that the police and Masters would fail to unearth it. Stella smiled bleakly. She had no reason to love H_2O or the Gunter girl. Quite the contrary. But for reasons of her own she was glad their love affair had progressed. It made many things easier for Stella.

The maid was just finishing now, patting this strand and that. Stella was staring at herself in the mirror, dissatisfied, and yet unable to pick any flaw in Elsie's work. Then it happened. Out of the corner of her eye she saw the bathroom door, back of her and to her left, open slowly, gradually, a half-inch, an inch! The mirror image was unmistakable!

THE ROSE BATH RIDDLE

TINGLY PRICKLES OF sheer horror chased themselves across the woman's shoulderblades. Her eyes slowly widened, but except for her right hand, she sat rigid. The maid, fussing and touching this and that, turning her head to eye the handiwork from this angle and that like a hen that has just laid a speckled egg, noticed nothing at all.

Stella's right hand crept down an inch at a time, and finally reached the sagging pocket of her negligée. Here was the flat, small bulk of a .25 caliber automatic, a weapon that had been in her hand ready for possible use more than once since the hour of Simon's death shrieks.

Waiting perfectly rigid and motionless even to her white-lashed eyelids, Stella made out the blur of a face and the glint of light reflected from a watching eye. She could not see the barrel of a gun pointed toward her; but it would have made little difference. She could not summon the strength to whirl about and shoot—or even to scream aloud. *This was one of the killers, there in her bathroom!*

Then the utterly unexpected happened. Just as black flashes of congestion began to appear on her retinas, results of holding back a shriek and the breath for it, until it went through her body like hot poison, the door slowly closed! Then came a click of the latch.

Elsie Fenlon started and looked up, but evidently decided that a breeze must have been responsible. She tripped a few steps away, and stood admiring her own work.

"There, you look wonderful, Moddom!" she breathed.

"Oh, yeah?" said Stella weakly. She tottered to her feet, keeping hold of the automatic in her pocket. Chill perspiration began to break out from every pore, and a trembling had come in her knees.

"Looks very nice," she said. "Now, Elsie, you go down and get me another pint of rye—the 1916 Overholt. God knows I feel I need it!" She had kept her voice from trembling, somehow, and was glad of the fact.

"Why, Moddom!" cried the girl, noticing her pallor. "Don't you want a glass of water first? I—"

"No! No water! Didn't you hear me? *Whiskey!* Get it *now!*" almost screamed Stella, stopping Elsie as the latter made two steps in the direction of the bath.

Of a mind that her ordinarily temperate mistress had suddenly gone loopy, the girl retreated hastily to the corridor, disappearing and closing the door behind her. Then Stella Mallen lifted out the little pistol, took it off the safety, and walked three steps toward the closed door.

"You may as well come out of there!" she said in a low, vibrant voice. "I saw you—Henry!"

There was no answer, no sound of the intruder.

Stella did not repeat her words. Instead, she crept noiselessly to the wall, holding the automatic ready on a level with her breast. Reaching over with her left hand, she seized the knob, turned it, and flung the door wide open, at the same time shrinking back behind the upraised pistol.

Nothing happened. It took a long group of seconds before Stella herself was convinced; but gradually, peering first through the crack between the door hinges, then little by little further into the white-tiled room itself, she knew.

There was not a person in the room!

Gasping in relief she darted in. The screens were in place on the windows, but one of the windows itself had been open for coolness. Stella quickly closed and locked this. Then she relaxed, catching the white porcelain washbowl for support.

At that moment her eyes rested upon it—a legal-sized envelope, fat with a folded paper, and bearing something typed as a superscription. It stood there, propped up on the handle of the medicine cabinet, where anyone entering would have to spot it immediately.

Her faintness gone now, she rapidly took the envelope and read:

LAST WILL & TESTAMENT
OF SIMON CORLAES

"My God!" Stella muttered excitedly. "I never expected to see that!" With nervous fingers she opened the unsealed flap, and drew forth the single, folded parchment sheet within.

One thing was instantly apparent. About a quarter of the sheet had been torn away roughly. Where Simon's signature and that of the two witnesses, Edward Green and James Leslie Walker should have appeared, the bottom of the sheet was missing!

For the moment that did not matter much to Stella Mallen. During a space of years she had often wondered—sometimes hopefully, more often with a cynical shrug—just what Simon would do in regard to herself. She had no right to expect more than she already had got from him, of course; and yet it was natural enough to wonder. Would he remember—certain things? Or would he be nasty at the end? Most of the time she had not bothered to speculate very long or deeply, since his health had been of the best. He might easily have outlived her, if he had not been murdered like his brother...

Now she smoothed the folds of the one single-spaced sheet, and read rapidly. Her breath caught in an exclamation of anger. The beast! The slimy, double-crossing little beast!

On sudden impulse she tore the sheet in two. Then she reached for a match, lighted it, and held it to both parts of the parchment. They burned. When the flames neared her fingers she wet the fingers of the other hand at the faucet, and took hold gently of the curling black ash. Thus she held the flaming parchment until the last bit had been consumed.

Crumpling the ash, she dropped it in the drain, and flushed it away forever.

"Beast!" she snarled again. At least one person knew now what had been in that hateful paragraph. That one person—was it really Henry Oliver, or was it Marshall Corlaes? And would he ever tell? The placing of the torn will in her bathroom looked a little bit as though blackmail might be intended. If that were the case, there was no doubt in her mind who it was that knew...

For the first time she noticed the smoke which hung in a blue blanket near the ceiling. A little was curling out into the boudoir now. Well, let it curl. On impulse she seized a piece of newspaper, crammed it in a tiny metal wastebasket, and set it on fire. After a moment she put it out with water. Might as well have an excuse for the smoke, if anyone should smell it and inquire...

Back in the room she paced up and down, her felt slippers making no sound. Then she stopped. Was it a board that had creaked just outside her door—the door which led into the hall? She crept close, and listened.

She put a hand to the knob, and suddenly flung the door open. A scowling man stood there, with his right fist upraised!

It was Henry Handley Oliver!

Stella screamed. Her knees caved, and she crumpled awkwardly forward, then rolled to her back, unconscious. The pin at the neck of her negligee came open.

When the heavy-footed policemen came running, they were not at all gentle in the way they handled Oliver. It did look bad for him, standing there dumfounded, over the unconscious body of a half-naked woman!

But when Connor dashed past, to investigate what had been going on inside the chambers there, he found nothing at all except a partly burned New York *Sun* in the waste-basket, and a strong smell of smoke in the air.

16

INQUISITION

"I TELL YOU, I just made a mistake! They told me to come up; Mr. Masters wanted me. I was kind of flustered, and turned to the wrong side of the hall. I was just going to knock on the door, when it went open—swish! Then Stella looked at me like she was seeing a ghost, and toppled over."

Twenty minutes had passed since Stella Mallen had fainted. Henry Handley Oliver stood before the long table in the living room of Simon's suite. He was pale, the freckles standing out like liver spots against the dead white of his skin. Connor and the two policemen who had pounced upon him in the hall had given him a taste of the oral third degree; and from the lieutenant's manner it seemed evident that more forceful measures would be forthcoming immediately. Connor did not believe any such story as Oliver had doggedly repeated over and over.

"How long have you lived in this house?" rapped out Connor. His tired eyes bored relentlessly into the prisoner.

"T-two years." Oliver wiped his forehead with one hand, pushing back the damp red hair which had a tendency to straggle down. "Two years and a month or so. B-before that I stayed down with the others at the big laboratory."

"And you want us to believe," said Connor, with crushing

irony, "that you hadn't ever learned which side of the hall your boss lived on? No, that doesn't go with me, young fella. Come through. What were you going to see Mrs. Mallen about *first,* before you let yourself be questioned by Mr. Masters and me?"

The laboratory assistant could only gape. He was troubled by a slight stammer; but now it was evident that his ideas stuttered worse than his tongue. "I—I assure y-you—" he managed to articulate.

At this point Jigger Masters slipped into the room. He had gone in with Elsie Fenlon, given Mrs. Mallen a drink of the rye whiskey the maid carried, and ascertained that the hostess had not been injured in any way. Leaving, he had sent for a police matron, and then had asked the maid to stay, with the hall door open part way, and a ready policeman stationed there. Mrs. Mallen had insisted upon dressing immediately.

Masters went over to the table, and whispered to Connor. The latter nodded and leaned back in his chair as if exhausted. The detective took up the inquisition, though not in the same line. As he questioned, Masters walked up and down, occasionally shooting a keen glance at the perturbed Oliver from hazel eyes, but most of the time thoughtfully scrutinizing the rug in advance of his steps.

"What we want from you first," said Masters in a measured voice, "is the full story of your work in gas chemistry—the process you invented, how Simon Corlaes got hold of it, and what brought about your employment here. In other words, *what hold did you have on Simon Corlaes?*"

"Oh!" The chemist was taken aback, and attempted to deny that there was any connection existing, other than that

"If you value your lives, people," he cried, "don't eat or
drink anything in this room! It may be poison!"

of employer and employee, between Simon and himself.
He stammered badly, and a flush rose, then receded again
from his countenance.

"Tell it your own way, then—right from the beginning,
when you first met Corlaes," said Masters dryly. "I doubt
that you'll be able to do much lying that will stick." He
nodded at the inconspicuous Barnes, over in a corner with
his notebook. "Of course we'll ask you to sign this statement when it's done. Anything false will bring about your
arrest as soon as we *prove* it's false!"

"Can I s-sit down?"

WHEN PERMISSION WAS given, the red-haired man
almost collapsed in a chair. Even then, he made a poor
witness, needing constant questioning and prodding
from Jigger Masters. He evidently thought at first that his
own work, and his importance to Simon Corlaes, could

be minimized; but the detective shortly disabused him. Masters, while not actually a research chemist, had been fascinated years before by the astounding discoveries made and utilized in the name of Simon Corlaes. He knew more about them, as a result, than many a professional chemist, and knew the sardonic fact that not a single one of the patents and secret processes which had rolled up additional small fortunes for Simon had been the product of the rich man's own brain.

The resulting story, yielded with manifest reluctance by Oliver, was that of a young chemical engineer who had a small income from a trust fund left him by his mother. He had done research in one of the old laboratories of M.I.T. in Boston, left untenanted for some years after that school of learning moved across the Charles to Cambridge.

These experiments had concerned themselves with the commercial possibilities of gases in the (so-called) argon group. Oliver had met with partial success. Through Simon Corlaes' laboratory had come news of an unimagined ease of handling certain gases in a liquid state. For several weeks Oliver had visited Corlaes—then returned to find that his own flimsy safe had been opened in his absence, and the results of his own work pirated!

There was no chance of proof. Though Oliver still knew his own work thoroughly and could reproduce it, the immense advantage of capital and all the needed equipment gave Simon Corlaes a start that rendered the situation hopeless.

"So I t-took a job with him," shrugged Oliver in conclusion. "I p-preferred to stay with my work, r-rather than just lose it all. He paid me a good s-salary."

"No doubt," said Jigger Masters. "But you had some kind of a hold over him. What was it?"

"Oh—w-well, he knew I knew he'd s-stolen my data. I threatened—"

"Oh, yeah?" put in Connor, seeming to awaken. "*What* did you threaten to do, stew him in some of his own gas?"

Oliver gulped convulsively. He was patently frightened and stuttered badly. In time they managed to get a denial from him, and a statement that he had threatened to sue for his just rights. This was nonsense, of course, since he had just admitted he would not have been able to prove any robbery or fraud.

"Of course that's not what you threatened," Masters put in calmly. "That would only have got you thrown out on your ear. Tell us!"

But the redhead stuck stubbornly to his thin story; so at last Masters changed tactics, scoring a black mark against Henry Handley Oliver.

"I suggest that you are on intimate terms with a young lady who was engaged to Simon Corlaes," he said. "You and he quarreled, didn't you?" That was a shot in the dark, but it had satisfying results. Masters had known only that suspicion had been cast upon the relations of this man with Eloise Gunter.

"Oh! Oh! Did Eloise—" he began, paling still more, and acting truly frightened. Then he seemed to realize the admission he had made, and leaned forward. "That wasn't anything, Mr. M-Masters. He didn't c-care a damn ab-bout her anyhow. He w-was only making me th-think he d-did. I didn't f-fall for his g-guff, and t-told him so. I t-told him if I w-were Eloise I'd st-tick him for b-breach of p-promise."

"Oh, so he'd broken with her?"

"Yes. N-no, that is, n-not exactly, b-but—" Stark terror had hold of the chemist now, for he realized how little chance there was that Eloise herself would not be forced to give her own version. And hers would be the whole truth as far as she knew it!

Masters gave him no time to collect himself. Plunging directly into the matter of a timecard for Oliver during the times that the murders had been committed, the detective wrung a stuttering confession from the terrified man that he "dud-didn't know wh-where" he'd been at the time Simon or Green or Haines would be slain. Apparently the only shred of an alibi he had was for the time immediately preceding the discovery of Kershaw's body—and a gleam in Masters' hazel eyes betokened that this was known to be of little value. Since no one knew at what time the rouge pot had been poisoned, Oliver's admission that he had been in and out of the house, and all over the grounds, left that matter decidedly open.

"Take him away, and hold him incommunicado somewhere," snapped Masters at last. "Particularly, don't let him talk to that Gunter girl. We'll have her up next."

"Oh, you c-can't do that. I d-demand a l-l-l-lawyer," stammered Oliver, afraid but furious now.

"No-o?" drawled Connor, slowly rising. He gave the necessary orders. "We'll see. Hold him until we know whether or not Mrs. Mallen will want to prefer assault charges. We ought to know that in a week or so," he said grimly to the officers who ranged themselves alongside

Henry Handley Oliver, and guided him firmly by the arms
as he left the room.

"IS HE REALLY the one, Jigger?" asked Connor. "He
certainly acts guilty as hell, but—"

Masters shook his head, taking out a cigarette and lighting it. "We're all through with surmises and working draw-
ings of this case," he said, blowing out a spill of smoke.
"There are parts of the evidence we need still missing. Call
Eloise Gunter."

Two minutes later the supposed fiancée of the dead
Simon appeared, glancing hesitantly into the room as
the door was opened for her by a uniformed man. She
was crisply dressed in a simple afternoon frock admirably
suited to her doll-like prettiness and manner of little-girl-
ishness. Her carefully mascaraed eyes were a demure and
calm shade of gray, that tint which pre-war poets called
violet, and showed no sign at all of weeping or worry. The
self-contained Miss Gunter probably had no intention of
letting a few off-stage murders bother her at all, Masters
derisively surmised. It would take something cosmic, like
forgetting to pack her bottle of golden hair wash, to do
that.

"Oh, do I sit here?" she cooed. "Just like a divorce case
witness? I'm thrilled. I pos'tively am! To think that you big
men would want to ask questions of little meeee…!"

With something almost like a giggle she arranged
herself in the armchair, crossing her knees, leaning her
chin on one elbow and tilting her head on one side as she
smiled up at Connor. The lieutenant looked disgusted.
He was too old and too tired for flirtatious witnesses. He
growled something over his shoulder at Masters.

It proved utterly impossible to pin Miss Gunter to a definite admission that she had been engaged to marry Simon Corlaes.

"Oh-h, no-o-o," she cooed airily. "I liked ol' Sime, he was such a dear. But marry him? I hadn't ever rilly thought much about it. I suppose I might have done. He was just a big, ol' bear, but he was nice to 'ittle me. I told him yes and then no, and then yes and then no—you know how 'tis." This with a dimpling smile to the glaring Connor. "But I didn't 'zactly love him enough. Mamie wanted me to marry him this fall."

Mamie, it developed, was Mrs. Penrhyn Gunter, her mother. Left a widow, comfortably fixed, she had been pinched slightly during the years of depression, and had developed a horror of poverty. Marrying her daughter to millions had become her one aim in life. This accounted for her complete collapse on hearing of Simon's death.

"I take it that you also kept a corner of your heart," said Masters, choosing words he felt sure Eloise must have learned in the talkies, "for a deeper, stronger love? One in particular, perhaps?"

"Oh, do I rilly have to answer that?" she bridled. But then she continued, not waiting for an answer. "Oh, yes! Always some big strong man. A woman always ought to rilly be in love with *some*one, oughtn't she?" And she looked up palpitatingly at Masters, who bowed solemnly—while gagging a little in secret.

It took time, but in the end Eloise Gunter was startlingly candid about Henry Handley Oliver. She loved him "pretty much." At first he had been jealous of Simon, but lately he had not been so insistent that she keep away from him.

Masters began to feel the stirrings of a hunch. What bearing it might have on the actual murders he could not fathom, but from the girl's manner he deduced quickly that in late months the thirty-year-old H_2O would have been by no means heartbroken to have Eloise marry her rich man.

"Then you'd probably have got a divorce from Simon, and married Henry some time later?" suggested Masters offhandedly.

"Oh-h, perhaps," she simpered. "One swallow doesn't make a summer. But I might have found somebody else beside Henry. He is always so serious."

"But Henry talked it over, and showed you how easy it would be to have plenty of money, and how you could induce Simon to give you a divorce when you wanted one. I suppose?"

"How did you know?" For the first time Miss Gunter looked disturbed. "That—that may have been the way. I rilly don't remember. But it doesn't matter now, does it? One can't be engaged to a dead man, can one?"

Masters ended with a few commonplace questions, then got rid of the girl as gently as possible.

"Deliver *me*," growled Connor, when the door closed. "Somebody ought to take and spank her good and hard. Idiot! Do we have to listen to any more sap-appeal silly-heads like her? I don't see it gets us anywhere."

"Well," drawled Masters, pouring out a cup of black coffee which now was only lukewarm, "I thought we might find use for Henry Handley Oliver before we were through. When you get around to it you might ask him again just what hold it was he really had over Simon that would make him so sure Simon later would agree to a divorce. I doubt that Henry will tell—now that his job is gone, anyhow."

Connor stared in a puzzled way. "What in hell has that got to do with it?" he demanded.

But Masters shrugged noncommittally, and asked the lieutenant to bring back upstairs the remainder of the people on Gildersleeve's list, one at a time, but in quick succession. He had small reason to think that any one of them would link up closely with the murders, and in that surmise he was right enough.

"They may add a little to our understanding of the general situation, though," said Masters, seating himself on the table edge, and sipping his coffee.

But with the exception of Mrs. Gunter, who was too ill for sustained questioning, each of the persons on Gildersleeve's list came in, answered queries, and departed, and with the exception of Black, who was guarded and suspicious of everything, none appeared to have much idea concerning anything that Jigger Masters wanted to know. The wholesale baker grudgingly admitted a sort of intimacy with Simon, but swore he could not guess who in the world would want to kill him. The others who were dead were all strangers to Black, though he "thought maybe he'd seen" Edward Green around the house once or twice.

IT WAS AT this moment that something like a tornado swept into the room. Casimir Sterling, District Attorney of Nassau, had been driven to activity by what he considered a horrible infraction of the rights of newspapers which usually gave him such welcome and warm publicity. Now he came, he saw, and he sputtered violently. Outrage, this jailing of reporters! Monstrous!

Casimir Sterling was a dapper, small man with an
eyebrow mustache, given to wearing a top-hat on any
reasonable excuse. He belonged to the wisecracking school
of lawyers and statesmen, but had grown bald before he
progressed to any genuine eminence, largely because he
lacked a sense of humor. His labored jokes invariably
caused acute discomfort to the few well-wishers he had
left.

Now he reached the place of inquisition, and came right
along in. And no less than sixteen reporters trailed right
along in with him.

In the ensuing confusion, Masters got the wholesale
baker out unnoticed, and then came back in, standing
with his shoulders against the door, listening with a grimly
satiric smile on his wide lips. Connor was catching the
hell he expected. The murders, it seemed, were the lieutenant's fault, due chiefly to lax handling of the case thus
far. What did Connor mean, putting reporters in jail for
merely following out their rightful work? What was the
big idea, anyhow, of allowing a bungling private investigator leeway in such a serious matter? Weren't the police
of Mineola, and the D.A.'s office, and the State Troopers,
if necessary, competent to catch a society killer?

For the first time the harassed Connor opened his
mouth. In a way he offered, then, his resignation.

"No," he said flatly, and shut his mouth again.

At that moment Masters felt rather than heard a knock
against his shoulder-blades. He went out, finding a policeman there, one Radburn whom Connor had instructed
to phone New York in regard to the early days of Stella
Mallen.

"Connor's rather busy right now," grinned Masters. "Can I take your message for him?"

"Sure," said Radburn, "only it'll take me maybe a minute or two to spill it. I couldn't get the whole thing certain sure, but it sounds funny to me."

"Fire ahead," bade Masters. "We're as near alone out here in the hall as we'd be anywhere in this house. What did you learn about Stella?"

Radburn tugged at his right ear and frowned. "I got it here—what there is of it," he said, taking out and thumbing open a small leather notebook. "First off, Stella Corlaes was the only child, when old Roger Corlaes married the second time. Her mother died when she was born, which was in May, 1896. She had a German nurse until she was ten or so. She went to school in Babylon, where the Corlaes family lived, them days, but didn't finish high school. She was sick a lot of the time."

"Hm. You wouldn't think it now."

"Naw, but she was a lunger, I guess—or maybe it was a nervous breakdown, like they said. One of them breakdowns girls get from playing 'round. Anyhow, she was took to that Bissell Sanatorium, or whatever it was, out to Sag Harbor. That burned down five-six years back.

"The funny part, there, Mr. Masters, just happened to come up. I know an old doc named Massman, a German who don't practice any more—he's so near blind he don't even read. He was on the staff out there at Bissell's, so I give him a buzz. Lives out to East Islip now, does Massman.

"Well, he started off by saying there hadn't never been no girl named Corlaes out there at Bissell's. It was only a small place, and he'd of remembered any rich girl, no foolin'.

"I insisted she'd been there, and left. Run off somewhere and got married, according to the tale that I s'pose you can get from her if you try hard. Massman didn't remember anything, though, until I got started jogging him. Spoke about Simon, and old Roger, and how Mrs. Stella Mallen was out here now. And *that* got a rise out of him!

"Mrs. Mallen! Why, he remembered her, sure enough! Such a young girl to be married, and in such terrible nervous shape. Now, Mr. Masters, catch your breath. When Mrs. Mallen had been a patient at Bissell's about four months, *she died!*"

Masters made no sound, but the hazel eyes suddenly narrowed, and he leaned forward almost imperceptibly. This was something entirely unexpected—Lord, but didn't it open new possibilities, though!

The policeman shook his head dazedly, wiped his forehead with one hand, and grinned. "That's the right dope, too," he added. "Anyhow, there was a death certificate signed for Mrs. Stella Mallen, aged sixteen years and eight months—a married woman that old!"

"What happened to her husband?" snapped the detective.

Radburn shook his head again. "Massman sort of had an idea there never *was* any Mr. Mallen," he said. "Hemmed and hawed—and it sounded to me like maybe that Corlaes girl was in trouble, and was sent out there under a fake name so's she could have her kid. Anyhow, there ain't any record of a marriage in New York, or out in Suffolk County, either!

"From then on, I dunno. There ain't any news about Mrs. Mallen, dead or alive, until after old Roger died, and she come out here to keep house for Alfred and Simon. How she c'd wangle that, being dead, I s'pose is what they got detectives for, ain't it, Mr. Masters?"

"*I* can add some to that—but not as much as I want to know!" said Masters grimly. "That was excellent work, Radburn. Keep it for Connor—and don't tell anybody else. The D.A. won't know enough to ask, for a few hours, anyhow; and by that time—"

Radburn grinned. Loyal to Connor, he admired the private detective immeasurably—and had no use at all for Casimir Sterling. Masters left him singing softly to himself.

17

EVERY MINUTE A DANGER!

DESCENDING THE BACK staircase, Masters found his chunky assistant Gildersleeve in the kitchens. Preparations for a pick-up supper were going forward rather spasmodically under Sorenson's directions. Nothing like a formal dinner would be possible, with the cook and maids so nervous they jumped when someone dropped a spoon on the inlaid linoleum. But the capable Sorenson kept his head.

"I thought mebbe there might be somebody want to mix mucilage with the mayonnaise, an' gum up proceedin's," grinned Gildersleeve in an explanatory aside. "So I come out, figurin' just bein' here might mebbe dilute or wash out kitchen crime."

"Good forethought," agreed Masters. "There's trouble brewing for tonight, I'm sure—but not out here, unless I'm horribly mistaken. You can tell Sorenson that I'm prepared to give him and the staff a clean bill of health. But tell him, too, that under no circumstances is he to allow any of the guests or members of the household out here, without informing me instantly."

"All right, Chief," nodded Gildersleeve. "Say, when do

we shave? You an' me c'd begin to qualify on the House of David team." He rubbed his bristled chin.

"About midnight—when this is over!" said Masters with grim emphasis. A glint of eagerness came into Gildersleeve's eyes.

"Grand!" he ejaculated. "But you really see a way? I'm farther off knowin' anything than I was when the whole business begun."

"I doubt that. You've been right into this up to your knees, Gil, and a great help. Now, there's one thing I want you to do. It'll take some persistence, I think—and you may get a punch in the jaw from a cop—"

"Huh? Just *one* cop?" chuckled Gildersleeve. He brought up one hairy fist, and looked at it with humorous question.

Masters smiled, but went ahead with directions. "At the time they carried Glendon upstairs unconscious, then waked him up partially and called Dr. Herschel, there was a policeman left with him. Glendon was out of danger, and had dropped into a normal sleep—or just about normal, anyhow. The cop saw that, and had an idea how he could be more useful. There was a shortage of men just at that time, before Connor got more men out of bed and over here.

"The policeman, therefore, went down and suggested to Connor that a guard at the head of the back stairs could leave Glendon's door ajar, and be certain of hearing him when he awakened. Also, that guard could keep an eye on the stairs and the whole length of that crosswise corridor."

"Sensible, wasn't it?" asked Gildersleeve.

"Um," said Masters noncommittally. "That policeman *may* have been in a position to see something we don't know about! Start with him from the moment he left the doorway to Glendon's room, and get down on paper every person he saw, and every little thing that happened—both upstairs and down. When you get it, with an approximation of the times, bring it straight to me.

"Now as you go, send Barnes back here to me. I think he's somewhere out front, writing or possibly typing out the statements he has taken down in shorthand. I have an errand for him. A little later will be all right on those statements."

A moment or two later the smaller assistant appeared, quiet, unquestioning as usual.

"Take a car and rip over to Mineola," bade Masters. "Get hold of Bathelsen, or any other one of the fingerprint men. I want you to bring a couple of blotters, and a fresh, damp positive—showing two or three prints of slender fingers. The sort of prints that might have been made by a man or fairly large woman. Hurry it."

"All right," acquiesced Barnes. "Any—er—preference as to whose prints they are?"

"None!" said Masters crisply. "Only, there must not be any file data showing on the print; no numbers or anything like that, you understand. Oh, yes, and you might bring back a pad and some of the paper used for recording new prints. It'll save me hunting for some—at a time seconds may be precious."

When Barnes hurried away, Masters walked forward into the east living room. Here, with one apparent exception, all the guests and Stella Mallen now were gathered, as well as those two quondam members of the family, Marshall Corlaes-Vandervoort and Lacey Glendon. Around the doors lounged four uniformed policemen;

but their relaxed attitudes suggested they regarded any strict watch on the small assemblage of people as a formality, nothing more.

AS THE DETECTIVE appeared in the doorway, looking about gravely at one and another, the half-hushed murmurs of conversation ceased entirely. White faces turned toward him, becoming haggardly tense again. To many of these people, the detective realized, the murders could not seem real. To the self-interested Eloise Gunter, for instance, who now sat with legs curled up under her on a long davenport, and pouting, there was probably only one tragic feature. Since Henry Handley Oliver had been taken to Mineola there evidently was no impressionable male on whom she could practice her baby-talk...

Lacey Glendon had dressed. Around his head he had wound a Turkish towel, turban-wise. There probably was cracked ice in this; for as Masters looked, Glendon took out a handkerchief and dabbed at his temples, where moisture escaped. His dark eyes were sardonic, their expression lowering from one angle, probably because of the "shanty" which partially closed the right one.

Mrs. Penrhyn Gunter half-reclined in a chaise longue, a green glass bottle of smelling salts in one dangling hand. Her eyes were closed, and the wrinkled face looked like a death mask. Near her moped the effeminate Lessington.

Stella Mallen stood with her back to the unlighted fireplace. She wore a plain black frock, rather severely cut. Probably a hold-over from the time of Alfred's funeral, Masters supposed. She half-smiled, and beckoned the detective, looking more at ease than at any time since the body of Edward Green had been discovered and the news spread. Likely she thought Harry Oliver guilty, and all the others safe because he had been taken into custody.

Jigger Masters nodded, but did not accept the invitation at once. He saw there was a tray of pink-colored cocktails on the serving table near Stella. The two Black sisters each had one, sipping it. They were seated together on the long bench of the concert grand piano, which occupied an alcove in the northeast corner, but facing away from the instrument. Their mother, Black, the baker, and the Carmichaels were in chairs grouped together at the other side of the room. Black had a stein of beer on a taboret at his elbow. LeFevre was not in evidence at first glance. He came in a moment after Masters' arrival, appearing in the short corridor which led from the lavatory.

Masters spoke. "I haven't seen you all together before," he said pleasantly, "but I just wanted to stop and tell you that Mr. Sterling, the District Attorney, now is in charge of the case. I think I may promise that everything will be cleared up in short order, and permission given for you to return to your homes. That is up to him, though, of course."

"Then Mr. Oliver really did it—the crimes?" called an excited feminine voice—one of the Black sisters.

Masters shook his head. "I'm not at liberty to say, just at present," he answered. "I believe that the mystery is pretty well solved, however. The police have a set of fingerprints they are very much interested in. It seems that the murderer wore gloves most of the time; but that just once he forgot, and touched something barehanded. A little slip, you know…" And shrugging, he walked into the room, going toward Stella Mallen. There was one person missing from the group, and he instantly worried about her.

"What became of Miss Graham, the dancer?" he asked Stella Mallen, shaking his head at two or three excited queries thrown at him by others.

"Oh, she's over there—in that chair—weeping for her maid," said Stella half-contemptuously, nodding toward a deep armchair which faced away from them, toward one of the north windows. As she spoke, Marshall Corlaes walked over, bent and asked some question in an inaudible tone.

Masters watched. It was evident that the young man received a reply, for he sat down on the arm of the chair, and spoke again. The girl still remained invisible.

"Did she tell you," asked Masters, "that the maid who was murdered was—her own mother?"

This startled Stella Mallen. "Her *mother!*" she exclaimed. "Oh, my God! Then—then I don't blame her for going to pieces like that!"

"Let's sit down here," suggested Masters, indicating a couple of unoccupied chairs off by themselves. "There are just one or two things I'd like to ask…"

"Well, I'll be gay and glad of your company, but I don't think I'll answer any questions," she returned with a smile. Her pale eyes watched him guardedly, however.

"I'll try, anyhow," he smiled. "For instance, just why did you and the Corlaes brothers agree that you were to assume the name of their dead sister?"

HE SAW HER fists slowly clench, and her body stiffen, but for the space of long heartbeats she did not reply. Her gaze was fixed on the tall figure of the turbaned Glendon, who now had moved over to the fireplace, and was scowling in their direction. But Masters thought Stella Mallen did not see anyone plainly at that moment. She was thinking disaster and—more than likely—murder, with himself as probable victim.

"Is—that—generally known?" she gritted forth from pale lips at length.

"The police told me. I don't think there has been any reason to inform the guests," he partially evaded. To his mind Stella Mallen was not guilty of the previous murders, though possibly she had knowledge of them. But there was no doubt at all she would consider the killing of a detective, if only her claim to the Corlaes estate could be preserved, as well as her social position among these people in Mineola and Biskra Harbor.

"It wouldn't do you any good to slaughter me. Come on, tell me all about it," he urged gently. "I'll see you through as well as possible."

She gave a harsh, croaking laugh. "Mind reader, aren't you?" she asked bitterly. "But I'm not afraid—now. I've lost all there is to lose, and I've still got a stake."

She paused, and seemed to ruminate bitterly. Masters waited, though he dreaded the inevitable interruption, from abovestairs. If only Casimir Sterling found enough up there to occupy him for another hour or two! Masters believed that by then he could present the district attorney with a solution to all the mysteries of Corlaes Manor.

"Yes, perhaps even a man—if you'd call him that," she went on in a more subdued voice. "But you don't care about my future—only the past, eh? Well, a lot of these smug people might be surprised—only I hope they won't be! I'd rather keep it dark, d'you understand?"

Masters nodded. He did not see how that could be done,

but perhaps Stella did. "I asked a question," he reminded her.

"Oh, yeah, so you did. Well, you knew I was in the Follies. Huh, did you go—and *remember* me?" she broke off curiously. "You must have been in knee pants!"

Masters nodded, smiling. "They were my first Follies," he said. "And I remembered you on the end. I saw you a few times after that, so your face stuck in mind."

"Mm, I didn't know us show girls had—*faces!*" she mocked. "If it had been a mole on my left thigh, now... But you ought to guess the dirt. I got hold of a rich sucker. Not Simon. I won't bother you with his name, because he was all right to me, and he's dead now.

"After he died I was stranded. Couldn't get a job except in burlesque. Simon came along, and so he was elected sugar daddy. Gave me a flat in town and all the fixin's. He didn't turn stingy till the last two-three years, out here.

"He was the one got the big idea. Him and Alfred had a lot of money, but neither one of 'em was married. They wanted to entertain, and sort of throw their weight around. So Simon signed me up to a regular contract—pure business, sayin' nothing about sex at all.

"Well, it worked out about as good as you'd expect. He got tired of me in time, and went after plenty younger girls; but that was okay by me. I'd got tired of him, too. Then Alfred was killed, and I just went on being a half-sister to dear old Simon—the dirty, double-crossing wretch!

"Ah, you'd like to know why I say that, wouldn't you? Well, I won't tell. Except this much. Just a couple or five minutes before Henry Oliver came around to kill me—or whatever he was going to do—he sneaked in the window of my bathroom! Yeah, he did! I s'pose because the maid was there then he didn't do anything. But didn't you smell his smoke? All devils smell of sulphur. Damn him, I hope he gets the hot seat—two-faced, sneaking thing! I hate that even worse than good, honest murder!"

As if unable to control herself longer, she arose abruptly, and strode across to the table where stood an array of cocktails. Selecting one, she tossed it down her throat. Glendon came up, but she snapped something, crossly at him, and with a shrug he strolled on.

Masters smiled thoughtfully. Getting her story simplified many things. Concerning the statement she had made that Henry Handley Oliver had visited her bathroom, Masters had a life-sized doubt. Just why had anyone wanted to go there? If it was to kill Stella Mallen, which might have been on the cards, it did seem that Oliver could have got at her much easier than by walking that stone coping around from the outside stairs, or from some other second-floor window. Question: *Had not Oliver been down-stairs at that time?*

No, Masters inclined to the thought that Stella was just guessing—perhaps trying to get some information on her own hook. There was another possible explanation; and the more the detective thought it over the less likely Stella's tale appeared to him.

MARSHALL CORLAES LOOKED up at that moment. Seeing that Masters was disengaged, he came over quickly and silently.

"Couldn't Miss Graham go to a hotel now?" he asked. "She's really all in; and since you've got H_2O—"

"Soon," promised Masters. "By the way, won't you sit

down a moment? Good. Did you know that that sock with which Edward Green and Haines were killed was one of a pair you owned?"

"Sock?" questioned the young man blankly. Then his features showed returning interest, and a coupling of ideas. "Oh, it was a sock, was it?" he asked slowly. "I suppose you *could* make a blackjack out of a sock…"

"Someone apparently did. And the sock was a gray one, badly shrunk. Do you remember telling me about such a pair?"

"Sure thing. I did have a pair like that, once. Lord only knows what became of them. I suppose they were stuck away in some drawer here. I haven't worn them for months and months—not since the last time they were washed, of course.

"What's on your mind now, Mr. Masters? Feeling a trifle dubious about it being Henry Oliver?" He smiled quizzically, but the eyes were searching and a little worried.

"I don't think Oliver had anything to do with it," said Masters quietly. "But don't pass that any further. I want you to take good care of yourself and Miss Graham. There might still be danger."

"The hell you say!" Marshall jerked about, and looked in the girl's direction.

"Not while we're both watching," reassured Masters. "But tell me a little about Simon. Did he have you and others in to watch his experiments—the ones he performed in his upstairs laboratory, I mean?"

"Oh, yes, lots of times. Before Oliver came I used to have to help. So did Lacey. It was fun, only—"

"Yes?"

"Simon got to drugging animals, and making them suffer. It wasn't as though he had been a surgeon, vivisecting for a definite purpose. Simon was plain cruel. I quit, and so did Glendon."

"Did you have a key? To the laboratory, of course."

"For a little while only. There were just two; and Simon made me give it back. Not that I wanted it, of course," he added hastily. "It was just that when he asked for it I couldn't lay hands on the darned thing. Finally located it in a top drawer of my chiffonier."

"Then you got pretty familiar with drugs—and with liquid air, I suppose?"

The youth's face grew deadly serious. "The answer is yes!" he said grimly. "I suppose that just about drives the last nail in my coffin, doesn't it? I tell you, Mr. Masters, there's a lot of evidence against me, I know. But I just simply didn't do it!

"If I didn't know for sure it was an impossibility, I'd pick your murderer for you. It ought to've been him," he added sulkily and ungrammatically. "Only, it wasn't. He was one of the victims, instead."

"Lacey Glendon?" asked Masters casually.

"Yes, you thought of him, too! Well—" Marshall hesitated. "He was in trouble over a bad check, a forgery. I heard that indirectly, anyhow. Maybe it had been all fixed up, though. Or maybe it wasn't even Simon he had the trouble with. Lacey couldn't have killed Simon, anyhow, so that fire's all out. I sure don't know who did. I'm just hoping against hope they don't try hard to pin it on me. They might succeed!"

Masters was grinning, though most of that grin was an

inward glow. The whole series of crimes spread out now before him, clear and well explained. There was only one great difficulty. Every clue of a tangible sort, every bit of concrete evidence in his possession, argued for the guilt of some person *other* than the actual criminal! The murderer himself had been fiendishly clever enough to see to that!

Only in the matter of motive was there a straight-away case. And even here the issue could be made doubtful and cloudy by a clever defense lawyer. Masters, in order that the State ever could secure a conviction, would have to prove prior knowledge on the part of the killer. Unless—

There was one other possibility. And setting his jaw grimly as he arose, seeing Gildersleeve coming toward him from the back of the house, Masters decided to chance everything on a single cast of the dice. If the worst occurred, and the killer played his hand pat with a defiant laugh, there probably would be no murders following the showdown, anyhow. And as it stood now, Masters quaked inwardly for the safety of at least two people in this room—possibly three!

A LITTLE CONFUSION delayed speaking to Gildersleeve. At the moment Masters arose, Sorenson and three serving maids entered with trays laden with plates, glasses, linen and silver. They took these to the serving table at one side, evidently preparing for another *al fresco* meal similar to lunch.

Then Masters nodded to Gildersleeve, drawing him aside. The stocky assistant presented a slip of paper on which were a few pencilled words.

"There weren't any punches exchanged, Chief," said Gildersleeve, "but neither was there much info. That guy

Kierney—the cop who was supposed to be watchin' Glendon—gets an idea reg'lar once every thousan' years. An' when he gets it, wowie! The earth c'd tremble like it does in a California fire an' it wouldn't shake *him*. Why, that blue-coated bufflehead got so sold on movin' a few yards down the hall, so's he c'd watch a little bit more hall an' stairs, that he chased Connor clear out to the highway—25A—an' waited there while Connor give directions to the gate-keeper! There was fifteen minutes or more when he wasn't watchin' *anything*! Now about them five-six people he allows mebbe he seen. He ain't ready to swear what any of 'em were doing, but—"

"That's fine!" interrupted Masters. "I don't care about the people. You got exactly what I hoped you—"

A tap on the shoulder caused him to bite off the sentence.

"Sterling wants you upstairs, Jigger!" a policeman announced. "The old boy's chewing spikes and spitting molten steel—so have fun!"

The detective stiffened. "All right. I'll be up," he snapped, then turned to Gildersleeve. "Watch these people while they're served and while they eat!" he directed in a low, tense voice. "Especially, keep your eyes on the plates of Miss Graham, Stella Mallen, and Marshall Corlaes. It may be hard, but I have to count on you, Gil. Every minute is a danger. I'd like to make them wait with this meal till afterward, but I don't know what the D.A. is going to do. May have to be with him for hours."

"I'll watch, Chief," said Gildersleeve seriously.

Masters had only to glance at the worn and utterly dispirited Connor, who slumped in a chair and stared at his bandaged right hand, to know just how Casimir Sterling was performing before his audience of sixteen grinning reporters. Owing to the manner in which they had been excluded from the estate during all this excitement, they were ready to pillory Masters and the lieutenant anyhow. With the chance to quote the district attorney's denunciation, it was certain that their comments would be scorching indeed.

"Ah, there you are," greeted Sterling, making a show of rearranging papers on the table before him—though what papers pertaining to this case he might possess was a mystery. "Come up here and have a chair. Now, I want to learn what your reasons may have been, if any, for leaping in here and assuming responsibility in the handling of a serious case. A *dreadful* case, if I may say so. And made infinitely worse by the bungling of you and Lieutenant Connor. Why, it might almost seem—it may seem to a court, in fact—that you positively *fostered* murder, in order that—"

"Excuse me, Mr. Sterling!" said Masters coldly, rising immediately from the chair he had occupied. "I take for granted that your denunciations already have been made. I won't listen to them. This is no time for personalities. Since you are legally in charge here, I shall be glad to give you everything I know in respect to what has happened. This should enable you to make an arrest soon. But I warn you, death still stalks this house! The murderer's job is not done—and until he is satisfied that—"

"What? You claim that there will be more killings, now I am here?" scornfully questioned Sterling.

"I hope and pray not," returned Masters patiently. "As I said, I shall be glad to turn over to you what I have unearthed here. But to my mind the danger is vital *right now!* I think I see how emergency measures may obviate it. But in the meantime I have no intention of telling what I know in front of members of the press. If you will dismiss them for the time being—"

"No!" roared Sterling, his face suffusing with angry color. He brought down one fist on the table for emphasis. "You seem to forget yourself, Mr. Masters. This case is coming right out into the open. And if you dare to think you can refuse to answer my questions, I warn you that there is such a thing as arrest and detention as a material witness—if not for actual complicity!"

"Then you may arrest and be damned," said the detective evenly. "I warn you, though, that if by stepping in by sheer strength and awkwardness this way you cause the death of"—he paused, and then held up fingers as he enumerated—"Mrs. Mallen, Miss Graham, or Mr. Marshall Corlaes, I shall have to—"

He got no further. From somewhere below sounded a heavy thump, then a confused clamor of shrieks and men's voices raised in shouts.

With a choked oath of horror and fright, Masters turned and ran for the door, and the back stairs at the end of the corridor. The murderer had struck again!

18

THE VALLEY OF SHADOW

UTMOST CONFUSION REIGNED in the drawing room.
The serving table had been overturned. Dishes and cups,
held in the laps of guests, had fallen to the floor. And down
at the west end of the room milled a huddle of men and
women, surrounding the prostrate figure of a girl over
whom Marshall Corlaes was working desperately.

At a glance Masters saw what he feared. The victim
was Dorothy Graham. Pallid, apparently lifeless, she lay
stretched on the rug, with the young man's arm supporting
her shoulders a little way from the floor.

"God grant it's not cyanide again," was the detective's
silent prayer, as he elbowed a way to the girl, knelt and
made a hasty examination.

Then his lips compressed. She still breathed! There
was none of the rigidity of cyanide poisoning—on the
contrary a limpness, and complete collapse. He looked at
her irises—partly retracted. Of pulse there was only a faint,
slow, and fluttering beat.

Masters knew that at best it would be touch and go.
He had to chance his diagnosis, founded as it was upon
slightly similar conditions observed in another member
of this household.

Disregarding the frantic questioning of Marshall Corlaes, he leaped up.

"Get the Nassau Hospital ambulance!" he commanded. "Someone get hot water—hot towels on her legs and arms. Glendon, come here!" He strode toward the tall figure of Simon's nephew. Glendon had shed his towel turban now, and his hair was dark with moisture from the ice pack.

"Quick, your hypodermic, man!"

"What? Are you crazy?" drawled Glendon, but his dark eyes flashed alarm. He stepped back, but too late. Masters grabbed him by the left arm, and with one savage gesture tore the lightweight jacket and silk shirt from cuff to armpit. Revelation! Just above Lacey Glendon's elbow the flesh was dotted with tiny purple marks, each one surrounded with a small, brownish halo.

"Your hypodermic—or shall I take it away from you?" cried Masters, furiously angry.

White-lipped but shrugging, Lacey Glendon reached back into his right hip pocket and brought up a flat, silver case.

Seizing this, and bucking through the reporters, now crowding wide-eyed to the scene, the detective sprinted again for the stairs he had just descended.

GAINING THE LIVING room where only Connor now sat, despondent, Masters twisted the knob which released the book shelf door, and ran into the laboratory. There was the long quintuple row of drugs and reagents atop the cascade liquefier cabinet. He ran his eyes sharply down the line, economizing seconds, and then seized a bottle bearing chemical symbols and the name *Strychnine Sulphate*. A fairly mild solution.

Opening this, plunging in the hypodermic, sucking up more of the liquid than it would be possible to use on a dozen patients, Masters swung about and retraced his steps to the drawing room at a dead run.

"Have to guess to save her life!" he gasped, kneeling down and taking her limp arm. He pushed out the air bubbles from the needle, then plunged in the slender steel. Only a couple of drops now...

Artificial respiration came then, with Masters straddling her slender body and working like a demon. Then, at the first gasp from her lips, he lifted her.

"Help me, Gil!" he cried. "Get her on her feet, and *make her walk!* It's her only chance! Here, Corlaes, you take my side. I want to be ready to give her another shot if it's necessary. This isn't a cure, only a chance to keep her alive till Nature conquers the drug. God grant she hasn't *much* of it inside her!"

"What in God's name is it?" cried the awed Casimir Sterling, who now was beginning to understand that the case he had regarded as a chance for airing some splendid denunciations of bungling private detectives still had ghastly possibilities.

"Aconitine poisoning, I hope!" snapped Masters. "Wait now, men," he said, halting the two who were walking Dorothy Graham. "Can you hear me, Dorothy?" He lifted her wobbling head, then shook her fiercely by the shoulders. "Wake up! Do you hear me? You have to walk! Come! Breathe deep! Now hustle her! Talk to her, Corlaes! Keep her alive if you love her! I won't give another injection just yet. Too much would be as bad as none."

Just a sobbing sound came from the girl, but for a couple

of minutes after that, while Marshall Corlaes cried out to her in a shaking, desperate voice, she seemed to manage her feet a little better, to understand that she had to do her best to help in this grim battle for her life.

The reporters now had reverted to type sufficiently so that some of them had out notebooks and were scribbling furiously. One, however, spying a cocktail resting on a chair arm, reached out for it, evidently intending to bolster his nerves.

Jigger Masters dashed it from his shaky fingers.

"If you value your lives, people," he cried loudly, "don't eat or drink anything in this room! It may be poison!"

"Oomagosh, and I was gonna—" shuddered the reporter. He turned greenish about the mouth corners, and licked his dry lips. A moment later he tore up some pages of shorthand notes. He, for once, thought the world at large might do without the excoriations of Jigger Masters uttered by Casimir Sterling, that renowned publicity hound. Only the word he used was not "renowned." His private vocabulary was more pithy.

During the ensuing twenty minutes of the fight for Dorothy Graham's life, guests, and even the remaining reporters, talked in whispers. Right there before their eyes was the awesome drama of a beautiful girl being dragged back from the grave time after time, through the ministrations and the will of three men.

They shook her till her head waggled helplessly on her neck. They shouted bullying insults at her. They even got down and hand-walked her dragging feet, when it seemed that she could not lift them for further steps. Masters slapped her upper arms, her shoulders, made her lift her head every time it slumped, spoke encouragingly to her when Marshall Corlaes ran out of breath.

But the effect of the sinister poison gained on them. The girl's face faded to paper-white, and beads of clammy weakness—perspiration started forth on her forehead. A vast lethargy gripped her—the sinking toward coma and the end.

DREADING THE MEDICINE which was her only hope, Jigger Masters postponed the second hypodermic as long as he dared, praying that a hospital doctor would arrive. But the time came when he was forced to administer a second injection of the enormously powerful heart stimulant. And he breathed a heartfelt sigh of relief when it was apparent she still had vitality enough to respond to it. For a little time then she walked with a surer stride, and even attempted a few strangled words. The detective, however, did not encourage her to talk. He adjured her time and time again to concentrate on the physical effort of walking up and down the room.

Masters saw the calf-faced Sorenson waiting with a circle of maids and the houseman Walker.

"Bring me an unopened bottle of brandy or whiskey, whichever is handiest," he directed the butler. "And a clean glass. I'm afraid of the strychnine," he explained in a lower-voiced aside to Casimir Sterling. "Going to try to keep her going on alcohol now."

"You're giving her *strychnine?*" gasped the district attorney. "But isn't that poison, itself?"

"Rather," said Masters grimly. "If the concentration is what I think it is, Miss Graham has had enough to kill two men! But *that* won't kill her, full of aconitine as she is!"

Fortunately there came an interruption. A white-coated physician carrying a bag, and followed by two men with a stretcher, came from the direction of the front door. Masters hurried over, and briefly described the presumed aconitine poisoning, and the measures he had taken to combat it. The doctor hastened over to the girl, and looked searchingly at her.

"Well, she's your case, Doctor," he said to Masters, making the natural mistake of thinking the latter a man of medicine also. "I couldn't do any more. She doesn't want a stretcher—be dead before we got to the hospital. Why not just keep her walking—yes, give her plenty whiskey," he added, seeing Sorenson proffering a pint bottle and glass.

Quickly Masters explained his status as a layman, earning a suspicious frown from the physician, but getting the latter to take immediate charge. On Masters' suggestion then they walked Dorothy Graham down to the west drawing room. A lavatory was handy there, and the doctor, with the stretcher men, could devote themselves to her care without disturbance from the others.

Masters caught the arm of Marshall Corlaes when he would have followed.

"Wait a minute or two," bade the detective grimly. "I have one piece of business to finish here, and I'll want every one of you present!"

Catching sight of Barnes, who had come in and was looking on wonderingly, holding two green blotters under his arm, the detective motioned for him to come forward.

Behind him appeared Connor, leaning wearily against the door frame, looking on with dull eyes as though this were some not very interesting motion picture through which he was forced to keep the role of spectator.

Telling Barnes to wait with the blotters, Masters grasped Casimir Sterling by the arm, and led him to Connor.

"I want you two men to cooperate with me just five minutes—and I think I'll be able to show you the murderer!" he said in a low, tense voice. "Not only the man who tried to kill this dancing girl, but the one who has been behind all of the crimes in this manor house!"

"Eh? Eh?" cried Sterling excitedly. "But I don't understand at all! You say you have him? Why not then—"

"You don't have to understand—yet. Just look wise, and back me up if I seem to need backing. Get your men around the doors and windows, Connor. Might have your gun ready. We're up against a man who will stick at nothing!

"He might have a gas bomb as last resort. If so, hold your breath, smash the windows, and clear out the people as fast as possible!"

"But what are *you* going to do? I must know before I can grant permission for any such—" began Casimir Sterling.

"Watch!" bade Jigger Masters tersely, and turned his back. The district attorney was left with his mouth open.

19

ONE OF US HERE IS GUILTY!

AS A PRECAUTION, Masters had everyone except the district attorney and the police sit down. Even Barnes and Gildersleeve seated themselves at ends of the serving table behind which the detective took his place, with the blotters holding the wet positive print, and the ink pad with papers. Some of the reporters who could not find chairs grouped themselves in the windows.

A hush of tense excitement and staring eyes! Masters, looking down sternly at the array of people before him, noted that Marshall Corlaes, who kept turning his head and fidgeting uneasily, alone was more interested in what happened in the other drawing room where Dorothy Graham was fighting for life. Masters resolved to let the boy go as quickly as possible. After all, he might be of service in keeping the girl dancer alive, if she still was in danger from the poison.

"Ladies and gentlemen," he began in a grave, clear voice. "For one of you, this is the end of sport. About nineteen hours ago Edward Green, a valet in this household, was done to death in his master's suite, by an intruder who used a makeshift blackjack as a weapon. Shortly after this, a man was killed outright, and another wounded in an identical manner—these happenings occurring in the garage behind and to the east of this house.

"Within half an hour after this was discovered, Simon Corlaes was murdered in a particularly shocking fashion, while taking a shower in his own bathroom. Doubtless this has been thoroughly described to all of you.

"Mrs. Graham, who acted as maid and dresser to her daughter, the dancer Dorothy Graham, was killed then. Also a warning was left for Marshall Corlaes, though that was never carried out."

For a moment the detective was obliged to stop. The household knew nothing, it seemed, of this threat against the young man. And all of them, presumably, still looked upon him as being Simon's heir.

"Mrs. Graham was killed by poison which was introduced into the facial rouge used by her and her daughter both.

"What seemed like an attempt on Mrs. Mallen's life was made—or, I should phrase it differently. We *thought* for a little while Mr. Henry Oliver might have been trying to kill Mrs. Mallen; but that is disproved now. Mr. Oliver will be set free with suitable apologies, this evening. After I have a talk with him!"

But the last words Masters said only to himself. He frowned down the district attorney, who moved as though he was about to protest any such high-handed proceedings with his only prisoner. For a wonder, the fussy Casimir allowed himself to be quelled—though with heavy mental reservations.

"At some time, probably quite early—although that point has not been definitely determined—another man was killed in a strange fashion, up in Simon Corlaes' private laboratory. That was Stanley Kershaw, a man who had suffered at the hands of Alfred and Simon Corlaes.

"Long before all this happened, too—I mention it, just because speaking of Kershaw reminds me—Alfred Corlaes was murdered. Oh, yes, it was called suicide at the time, but we have reason to think differently now. The same killer was responsible, though we cannot make him pay the penalty more than once, unfortunately.

"Lastly came this sneaking, dastardly attempt upon the life of Dorothy Graham—a person who never before set foot on Long Island, until she came to entertain at Mrs. Mallen's party! We all hope, of course, that she is now feeling better, and is out of danger.

"With this much preamble, I will get to business. In all his skulking operations, with one momentary exception, our killer wore gloves. He left no fingerprints at all—save on this one occasion."

"Then there *was* one!" broke in Casimir Sterling tensely.

"There was indeed! You are too lately arrived to have heard everything, Mr. Sterling. But Lieutenant Connor knows. His men discovered the prints.

"I want you all to mark this carefully. The story is too long to tell in this moment, but you may take my word for it, the prints we have will name for us the murderer, just as surely as the sun will rise tomorrow! They were left at a time and in a place which makes certain no one but the murderer could have made them. We have made absolutely sure of that! Now, it is my feeling, that *one of us here is the murderer!*"

A GASP, AND half-hysterical giggle, quickly smothered,

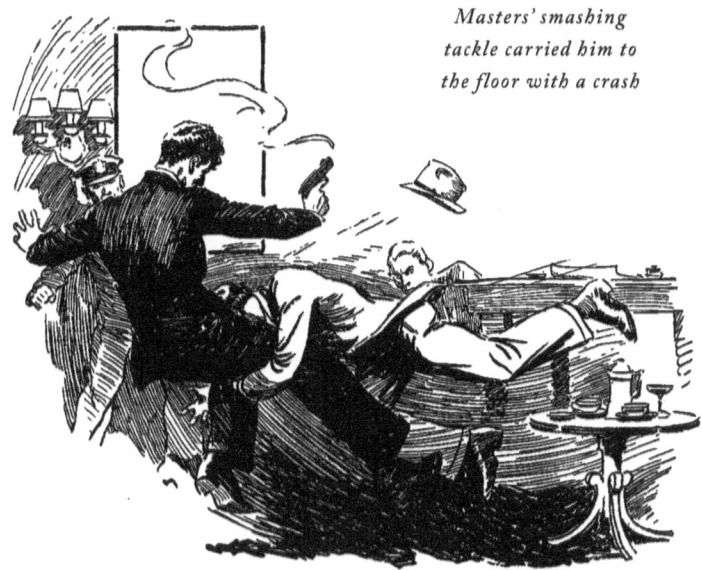

*Masters' smashing
tackle carried him to
the floor with a crash*

came from Stella Mallen. In that breathless moment it was a horrid sound, but Masters paid no attention.

"I have a photographic duplicate of the incriminating prints here," he continued, lifting one of the green blotters, and showing the damp positive. Two enlargements showed plainly there on the glossy paper.

"I am going to ask the men here to come up, one at a time as I call their names. Each will register the prints of his right hand. From those prints we will name the killer!

"Of course," he added as a significant afterthought, "if anyone sees fit to refuse, there are means of forcing him to comply!" He nodded at the policemen, who were watching with tense interest.

"All right, Mr. Marshall Corlaes, will you step up? Thank you. Your fingers against this pad… then on this sheet of paper. Now will you go back to your seat?"

With a small magnifying glass Masters bent over the new set of prints, comparing them with those on the damp

positive. He took his time, making sure there was no simi-
larity.

He straightened, shaking his head. "Utterly different—
no points of agreement at all!" he announced. "Mr. Corlaes,
you are assuredly innocent. If you wish, you may go now to
see how Miss Graham is getting along."

"Thanks!" breathed Marshall huskily. He vanished in the
corridor leading through the house.

"Mr. LeFevre, you are next!"

For some reason the French-Canadian was shaking visibly, and his swarthy skin had gone ashen. Yet the voice in
which he answered was clear, and rather haughty.

"I left my right arm at Ypres, sir!" he replied. "And
besides, I did not know half of these people who are dead.
Why should you suspect me?"

"There is no question of suspicion. This is *certainty*—one
way or the other! Let me have the prints of your *left* hand,
Mr. LeFevre!"

Masters knew it was mummery, but he went through
the proceedings with grave deliberation, just the same. If
the killer possessed high-strung nerves, this was the most
deadly test which could have been devised.

After LeFevre, Leland Stamford Lessington was examined, and duly dismissed.

The financier, Carmichael, was called. He went through
the process without comment, waiting at the table, and
then shrugging briefly as he was allowed to return to his
seat, cleared of suspicion.

Each time now, the audience held its breath during the
examination of the prints; and each time, the exhalations
of relief were audible.

Masters called the baker, Black. That stodgy individual arose and waddled to the table, irascibility and knowledge of innocence struggling for expression. Veins showed on his temples from the effort of repression.

"Ach Gott, du bist ein Dummkopf!" he burst out, using a language he had not spoken in public since he had been Herr Schwartz, back in 1917.

Masters took his time, however. In the end he admitted gravely that Mr. Black was not the murderer, and was rewarded with a somewhat beery snort of indignation, as the baker waddled away.

Masters waited a full four seconds, until the smiles faded.

"And now," he said, his voice deepening with menace. "Now it is your turn at last, Mr. Lacey Glendon. Will you please step forward and let us see the prints of your right hand?"

There was the cast of the dice, Masters' desperate gamble. It could be carried only a little further now. Either Glendon would crack, or—

Glendon cracked!

"I think you lie about those prints!" he cried hoarsely. "But what the hell—you *know!* Sure, I did it!" His voice rose in timbre almost to a scream. Suddenly he tossed something into his mouth, gulped once.

"I killed 'em! Now—*keep back!*" He yanked forth an automatic pistol. "This poison I've taken finishes a man in fifteen seconds! Fifteen seconds—eight shots—I'll take some of you meddling devils along with me to hell!" He swung the muzzle of the blue weapon in the direction of Jigger Masters.

Whammm!

Connor was the only person in the room who could fire without endangering an innocent person—and he shot, lefthanded. The bullet no more than tipped the shock of wet hair on Glendon's head, passing on to smash a pane in one of the oriel windows behind him.

But Glendon flinched, just as he fired. His bullet scored the top of the table which Masters vaulted, passing directly under the detective's body without touching him.

There came a second shot, even a third from the deadly automatic! But Masters, only touching the floor beyond the table, leaped again in a long, smashing tackle which carried Lacey Glendon backward to the floor with a crash.

Then police piled on top of the two men, and Gildersleeve, raging at the hurt he knew Masters must have received, wrested away the smoking pistol before a fourth shot could be sped to an unaimed destination.

Under the figures of four husky men, Lacey Glendon's body suddenly convulsed. A rattling scream burst from his throat. "Cyanide—*awful!*" came his last, piercing words. Then diminishing convulsions, rigidity. And Lacey Glendon, murderer, was dead.

A little pale, tightly gripping his right thigh where blood welled slowly from between his fingers, Jigger Masters was helped to his feet.

"Cyanide!" he said. "Well, it was best—perhaps for all. I remember once my chemistry prof said to the class, about that poison, 'It only takes a few seconds to work, gentlemen; but I envy nobody what happens to him *during* those seconds!'"

20

SIMON THE JESTER

THE SOUND OF shooting brought Marshall Corlaes on the run from the west side of the house.

In the milling confusion he made straight for Masters. Tears had been streaming from the young man's eyes, but they were tears of happiness.

"She'll live, Mr. Masters! She'll *live!* And I have you to thank!" he cried. Then he noticed something wrong. "You were hurt? It was Glendon, after all? How badly did he get you?"

"Easy does it," grinned Masters. "This isn't much. The bullet went right on, missing bones and all important blood vessels. I'll just need a tight bandage when your doctor in there is free. So your lady really is making it! Doggone it, I'm glad!"

He held up one hand for the youth's convulsive clasp. Secretly Masters had become suddenly afraid that Marshall might go Gallic and kiss him. But the strong grip was enough.

"You know, one of these days," suggested the detective, "if you hadn't anything particular in mind to do, you might come around and have a talk with me. My work is getting rather hard to handle, and I might be able to use a third assistant."

"Sold!" cried Corlaes joyously. "Oh wait. I've got to tell the news to someone!" And he dashed away.

"Bet he forgets the doctor," said Masters with a chuckle.

Barnes and Gildersleeve had not forgotten, however. They brought the medico, and carried Masters upstairs to the room previously occupied by the dead murderer. Here the wound was examined, cleansed and bandaged.

"Barring infection, it should not amount to much," said the doctor. "But you will have to go to bed with it a few days."

"I'll be all ready for bed—and various other luxuries— as soon as I finish up a couple or three little things here," grinned the detective tiredly. "First off, Gil, tell Connor to bring me Henry Oliver. He's to be released, of course, but I want to learn a thing or two from him before anyone tells him that.

"Meanwhile, I'll have a chat of the same nature with Mrs. Mallen. Oh, yes, and before she comes here, be sure to have Sorenson clear away and throw out all the food and drinks that were served tonight downstairs. And I'd like a freshly made pot of black coffee.

"Barnes, I want you to find Sterling and Connor. Tell them that as far as I am concerned, all of the guests are free to depart for their homes. All of them who are curious enough, though, may stay. About ten o'clock I'll come down and give my version of this affair. Before that I'm going to have a smoke in peace. I don't want to be pestered by reporters."

Despite some impatient mutterings on the part of the

district attorney, who realized now that he had come too late for any personal kudos in this case, the program was carried forward in this fashion. Masters held brief conferences with Stella Mallen, then with Henry Handley Oliver. Both left him looking disgruntled, having told bits of scandal they had intended to keep locked in their own brains.

Of all the crowd downstairs, only Black the baker took advantage of the permission to depart. He waddled away in high dudgeon; but his wife and daughters stayed. In order to make room for everyone, practically all the chairs of the manor house were lined in rows in the east drawing room. Masters would occupy a chaise longue which had been raised on four ottomans for the occasion.

By half-past nine all was ready. But then came an odd interruption. With all the people, police included, standing about, some drinking freshly opened wines or liquors, many of them acting a trifle silly with release from the terrific tension, a new arrival came to the house, and stood framed in the west corridor doorway, staring about him with open-eyed astonishment.

"Heavens above! I surely never expected a *party!*" he exclaimed in a squeaky voice.

All eyes turned. They beheld an extremely fat little man in evening clothes, looking something like a spinning top, with his small head, seeming lack of neck, and corpulent body tapering down to very tiny feet.

"Jellybean Binney!" choked Stella Mallen, having a hard time keeping back the hysterics which had been all too near release for more than an hour. "Simon's lawyer!"

But then she got control of herself, and went through the motions of hostess. She explained quietly to the lawyer what had happened, and suggested that he go up and talk to Masters. This suggestion seemed to meet the little man's approval. He went quickly toward the staircase.

"That's old Binney, isn't it? The shrewdest probate lawyer in New York," asked and commented Carmichael, who was at Stella's elbow.

She stared. "Yeah, it's Binney," she answered slowly. "And I'm Stella Mallen, Queen of the May!" With which she walked over and almost fell on the davenport. It had been a long day, even for the nerve and strength of an ex-Follies girl. When Jellybean Binneys got rated as shrewd lawyers, almost anything at all might be expected to happen.

At five minutes past ten Masters was carried down; and with him came the fat little lawyer, carrying his own chair, which he placed inconspicuously off at one side. While the detective's wounded leg was being made comfortable with pillows, there came a blanket-shrouded figure, carried from the west corridor in the arms of Marshall Corlaes.

The figure in blankets was Dorothy Graham. Masters saw her and smiled, raising one hand in congratulation and welcome. She was able to smile back, though waving was impossible, as both arms were held beneath swathings of blanket. Even yet it was necessary to preserve every particle of precious bodily heat.

Marshall Corlaes did not put her down. With one rather defiant glance about, he accepted a deep leather chair, and sat down with her in his arms.

WITHOUT FURTHER DELAY then, Masters spoke:

"Friends," he began in a resonant, businesslike voice, "tonight ends the most terrible case with which I have ever been connected. For almost all of you it has been a ghastly day of dread and horror also.

"I shall bring it to a conclusion now, trying to explain each step in the extraordinary series of crimes which took place.

"The chief reason why it has been so hard to grasp quickly, and impossible to prevent deaths which never should have occurred, lies in the fact that like most planned murders, the one murder here which made necessary all the rest of the crimes, had roots deep in the past.

"In the first place, here was a small, compact, family group—I have found no near relatives besides the dead murderer, Lacey Glendon. Neither Mr. Marshall Corlaes, as he has been known, nor Mrs. Stella Mallen, is a relative of Simon Corlaes at all! What and who they actually are, I shall explain in due course. Some of this will be regarded as scandal, I suppose, but it cannot be helped."

Here there was a hum of half-shocked surprise, but it quieted at once when Masters raised his hand.

"As I said," he continued, "it was a small family group, and one which rose from financial obscurity to immense wealth in the short space of thirty-five years.

"This wealth was obtained in various ways. Part of it came from the stock market—perhaps the greater part. Some of the rest was piled up through the commercial-ization of gas processes. Many of these, if not all of them, were stolen by the three Corlaes men—old Roger, Alfred and Simon, his sons.

"Naturally, many men had just cause to hate the family. There were other reasons for this hatred, too, besides the stolen gas processes, but I need not go into them. They played little part in this case. As a matter of fact, the bare-faced robberies of Alfred, Simon and Roger Corlaes accounted directly for only one of the murders, that of Stanley Kershaw. But in a way there is little doubt that because so many men hated, and so many men wished the death of Simon Corlaes, his actual murderer got his inspiration from the atmosphere of this place, so to speak.

"About one year ago a ne'er-do-well nephew of Simon and Alfred, Lacey Glendon by name, awoke to the fact that he was the only actual surviving relative of these men. He had learned two things. First, the young man whom Simon had expected to adopt—though Alfred's opposition delayed the actual legal steps—never had been adopted.

His name was Marshall Corlaes only by lip service. It actually was Marshall Vandervoort, and he was the son of a man whom the Corlaes family had despoiled. So, he could not inherit the estate, provided Alfred and Simon died intestate.

"As a matter of fact, Alfred willed all he had to Simon. So far that was perfect. I have no doubt at all that Alfred did not commit suicide; that he was murdered by Lacey Glendon.

"The mysterious hourglass in that case does not make any sense. It probably was just in front of Alfred's body through sheer coincidence. It gave the murderer an idea for future use, however.

"Those among you who are following my remarks, right now are thinking of Simon's supposed half-sister, the woman you have known as Mrs. Stella Mallen. Why should she not inherit?

"The reason lies in the fact that her name is Lettie

Bow—no relation to Clara. When Alfred and Simon grew rich, they began to aspire to something of a social life. Of course anything like genuine society was impossible to them; yet they managed a serviceable imitation, entertaining in this manor house.

"Simon signed a business contract with Miss Bow, whereby she was to assume the name of his half-sister, dead many years, and act as their hostess. This was carried out with no great hitch for over nine years. But of course Miss Bow has no rights in the estate, beyond the possibility of receiving a bequest in Simon's will."

"And I can do without *that!*" came the woman's strident comment.

"We shall see!" smiled Masters. Then he proceeded:

"So Lacey Glendon, having murdered Alfred, would stand to inherit the Corlaes millions, provided only Simon Corlaes died intestate.

"Everyone knew, however, that Simon had drawn a holograph will, the provisions of which he let the possible · beneficiaries know would be found freakish and unpleasant to anyone having expectations.

"He kept that will up in a wall safe in his suite. Anyone who knew the combination, or who was a bit clever with a hairpin, was welcome to go in and peruse it. Lacey Glendon learned the combination, of course. He believed it necessary to steal and destroy the will, you see."

"Much against my principles and judgment," piped up Binney then, "I was compelled to spread that news for Mr. Corlaes, letting everyone here know about the will."

"We understand, Mr. Binney," nodded Masters.

"Oh, so that was the way of it!" said Lettie Bow, under

her breath. She looked with heightened interest at Jelly-bean Binney, but he stared coldly back at her.

"THEN," CONTINUED MASTERS, ignoring this by-play, "Simon's death was scheduled. Glendon planned with devilish ingenuity, intending—exactly as the murder actually was carried out—to freeze Simon to death with liquid air, at the very time his victim was taking a hot bath!

"Normally that happening never in the wide world could have been suspected—by myself, or any other investigator, I feel sure. But there was a complication. The killer was cramped for time. I must explain this, before going back to take up the actual time-card of the crimes as they occurred.

"Lacey Glendon was a dope addict, a drunkard, and a failure in business. He had no principles at all. When his debts grew intolerable, he took advantage of a certain carelessness in Simon's habits. Lacey Glendon forged Simon's name to a check for five hundred dollars.

"That was months ago. We know about it only because Simon raised a fuss at the bank, and then discovered, three months after the check had been cashed, that there had been such a check which he had not written—according to his best recollection, at any rate.

"Glendon managed it this way. The canceled checks were mailed out monthly by the bank. Glendon knew the date of that mailing. He intercepted the postman, and got the mail that day. Since he was a frequent visitor, the postman did not question his right to take the mail.

"Glendon burned up that whole envelope of checks. Simon, being somewhat careless, did not notice this until much later. And by that time, no one at the bank remembered who had cashed the five hundred dollar check.

There was no possible way of tracing back, so Simon let
the matter drop.

"Glendon went further. He was going to kill Simon
some time, but meanwhile he had to have money. So he
forged a check again, this time for ten thousand dollars!

"This time he was caught, the bank people not being
entirely dumb. Simon raged. He threatened prison, but was
persuaded to allow Lacey Glendon a day or two to make
good on the check.

"Glendon in turn persuaded Lettie Bow—the Mrs.
Allen you knew—into helping him. She pawned a blush
pearl necklace for eight thousand dollars, the amount
needed to complete the ten thousand, since Lacey had
two thousand left of the forged check.

"Now to our murders. At some time last evening Simon
probably decided that he would not be content with resto-
ration of the money, but would send Lacey Glendon to
prison as well.

"In some way Lacey Glendon found out this; that he
had to divert the mind of Simon Corlaes from prosecution.
So he decided to warn Simon. The latter was a physical
coward. If threatened with death he probably would not
be able to think of anything else for the time being. The
actual murders probably were not scheduled for any time
as crowded as this one, with scores of people and servants
on the grounds. But Lacey Glendon saw rich opportunity,
as he thought, and snatched at it.

"Now, take a deep breath. Since you understand the
complex motives which actuated these people, I shall start
in with the crimes themselves. I may say that this recon-
struction is the product of complete elimination. No one

else but Lacey Glendon *could* have done the deeds—*all* of them! Therefore, how did he accomplish them, while seeming to have the very best of alibis?

"First, he appeared at the lawn party, strolling about here and there. His absence would not be noticed in particular.

"When he went upstairs in the manor house, he may merely have intended to place the warning in Simon's room. He overlooked the possibility of Edward Green waiting there. But Glendon was a real genius in crime. He adapted himself easily to the unforeseen, actually making use of many happenings which would have floored a lesser man.

"He found Green in the living room of Simon's suite. Carrying a sand-loaded sock—a sock which belonged to Marshall Vandervoort, just as an artistic touch—Glendon used it to kill Green. Then he typed the warning message, leaving it propped up on an hourglass. The dead body, of course, would make that warning doubly impressive to Simon.

WORKING FAST THEN, Glendon opened the safe, and to his delight found not only the will of Simon Corlaes, but also the forged check which he had written and cashed. He took these, and left the manor house, appearing again on the lawn. Likely he was not absent more than ten or fifteen minutes in all.

"It is probable, however, that during this time he killed a second man—Stanley Kershaw. Wounded him, I should say, for Kershaw partially recovered, and did not die until hours later.

"The actual circumstances do not matter much now, though until I discovered the fact that Kershaw had lived some hours after being stabbed, I thought Lacey Glendon must have a genuine alibi.

"What probably occurred was this. Glendon knew of a bookcase door into the laboratory. He took one look into that place, just to make sure no one possibly could have heard or seen anything. And to his amazement he found Stanley Kershaw lurking there!

Knowing how Kershaw had been bilked by the Corlaes family, I have little doubt that he, too, was hoping for a chance to kill Simon Corlaes.

"But Glendon hit him with the sock, and dazed him. Then, grabbing up a spear file which stood on a laboratory table, Glendon stabbed him, lifted his body, and placed it in one of the two fume-hooded vats, jamming down the cover so tightly it wedged around Kershaw's forehead. As I said, the neck wound caused Kershaw's death some hours later.

"Meanwhile a new and extremely clever idea had come to Glendon. Why not go through with his entire plan, and do it in a fashion which would make it seem certain he was not only innocent, but one of the victims?

"When the story of Green's murder did break he left instantly. Probably he went to the house first for a grim purpose, that of poisoning the dancer's rouge. She had become a menace to him, you see, for she alone could implicate him. She knew that someone needed that eight thousand dollars; and if she squeezed Lettie Bow, it is certain that the latter would tell to save herself. So Glendon poisoned the rouge to kill Dorothy Graham, and killed Mrs. Graham instead.

"He hurried down to the garage then, just before the police got to the house. In the garage he struck and killed

Haines, the chauffeur. Then he pounded himself above the eye, making a visible bruise, and cutting the skin slightly with a ragged fingernail, so there would be a little blood.

"This was a real touch of criminal genius. He injected into his own arm, using his hypodermic, a tiny dose of a powerful drug, aconitine—the same one which nearly caused the death of Miss Graham. This is a vegetable alkaloid which slows the heart and dilates the blood vessels. When Simon Corlaes and I found him floundering there on the floor of the garage, his condition was exactly what one would expect to find in a victim of a blow on the head.

"The small dose of drug would wear off in time, of course. From then on Lacey Glendon was fully capable of sustaining the deception, though. He was a good actor.

"Everything worked out even better than he had dared expect. Instead of being shipped to the hospital—Simon's penuriousness accounted for that—Glendon was taken upstairs and given a room. So then, as soon as the policeman watching him left, Glendon went across the hall, entered the laboratory, and doubtless listened to what we were saying in the living room of the suite.

"Then he heard Simon start to take a shower in the rose bath cabinet! That was the killer's opportunity! He shut off the water, turned on the liquid air, and then reversed the process. He had the Onnes flask detached and back in the cabinet, probably in less than two minutes' time.

"Then, watching his opportunity, he mingled with the crowd in the corridor, probably feigning dizziness, and finally went back into his room to seem still overcome. He very nearly got away with it, too. Probably if he had been content with that, he might have done—though I surely would have suspected.

"From that time on, Glendon was watched by someone—except for a short period when I had Barnes lock him in his room. He was supposed to be asleep then, but wasn't. He bolted his own door from the inside, and climbed along the ledge—only a distance of about eight feet, there—to the window of Lettie Bow's bathroom.

"Since Lettie held that dangerous information in respect to the check forgery, I think there is no doubt he wanted to kill her; would have done, if she had been alone. However, Glendon found the maid, Elsie Fenlon, working on her mistress's hair. So he left the will, all except the signatures, which he had torn off and destroyed at the time he destroyed the forged check.

"Likely that will was to have thrown suspicion in Stella's direction, but it did not work that way. Stella, or Lettie, rather, found and burned it. She tells me that in it Simon was obnoxiously frank concerning his household and all his supposed friends. So it is small loss.

"One of the men against whom Simon was especially virulent, was Henry Handley Oliver. That was natural enough. Henry, whom all of us have suspected to greater or less extent, was finally let out because his motives all pressed in the opposite direction. He had a soft seat right where he was, as long as Simon stayed alive. He had a good job, he was on terms of unofficial intimacy with Simon's fiancée, and he had a hold over both Simon and Stella Mallen. He used that hold, which was a knowledge that for years the relation between Stella and Simon had been something more than brother and half-sister, for blackmail.

I suggest that Mr. Henry Oliver is perhaps the least to my taste of all the people connected with this grim business. But as I say, it is not my place to moralize.

"There was just one more thing. No doubt Lacey Glendon, being caught in the net of circumstances like many another killer, would have liked to do away with Dorothy Graham and Marshall Vandervoort, as well as Stella— Lettie Bow. He tried, and nearly succeeded in his second attempt with Miss Graham, as we know.

"But then came the end, which you all saw. The inevitable end. I think, my friends, that is everything." Masters reached for a cigarette, and lighted it.

"OH, NO, NO," called Casimir Sterling, above the voices raised in comment and congratulation. "You missed one important thing, I think. Yes, yes, you did. Just where and when did Lacey Glendon leave those two incriminating prints you showed?"

"He *didn't* leave them!" admitted Masters, smiling. "Those prints were left originally on the glass windshield of a sedan, over on Jericho Turnpike. They were made by a notorious young murderer, who was duly electrocuted for his crimes, some time ago.

"I just borrowed the prints from your department. I was taking a chance on bluff. I had no genuine evidence, but I thought I could bluff a gambler. Glendon was a man with imagination, and a chronic gambler. The bluff worked. If it hadn't—well, I hate to think of it! Let's not!"

And with that he turned with a smile to the dark, lovely eyes of Dorothy Graham. Still carried by Marshall Vandervoort, she had come to give her thanks to the man who had saved her life.

Masters flushed, and grinned. "Never mind that, you two. I like you both. Be happy. Oh, yes, and Marshall, there's one thing that won't become public property until after the funeral of Simon Corlaes. But I'm going to give you a little warning. You'll have some thinking to do. *Simon Corlaes made a second will!*

"Yes, that's true! Binney told me. This second one was serious, and its provisions are intelligent, not spiteful. There are a number of bequests—among them, one of $100,000 to Lettie Bow—but you, Marshall Vandervoort, are named as residuary legatee!

"Wait! Don't say anything until you've had a long time to think it over, and the advice of the best lawyer you can find. I—uh—suggest Binney. Also, my own thought in the matter is this. You will receive in due course something like twenty or twenty-five million dollars, perhaps.

"Now, consider that there is no doubt but Simon Corlaes defrauded your own father of a fortune. Also, he—I am using Simon as a symbol for all the activities of his father, brother and himself—cheated others. Why don't you see to it that the others, or their heirs, are reimbursed—and then keep the rest for yourself and your nice wife with a clear conscience?"

"I'll do that, Mr. Masters!" cried Marshall impetuously. "That's the best ever! But—but I—hell, do I still rate that job you spoke of? I haven't anything in the world to do, you know."

"Well," smiled the detective good naturedly, "come and see me if you want me to—after you've had a good long honeymoon! And now be happy together, children!"

www.ingramcontent.com/pod-product-compliance
Lightning Source LLC
Chambersburg PA
CBHW030544030726
47495CB00004B/1119